D1634189

Rocky and The
Black Eye Mystery

by the same author

STREET OF THE SMALL NIGHT MARKET
FROG IN A COCONUT SHELL
THE LOSS OF THE 'NIGHT WIND'
A SNAKE IN THE OLD HUT
DARK RIVER, DARK MOUNTAINS
A PAIR OF JESUS-BOOTS
A PAIR OF DESERT-WELLIES
ROCKY AND THE RATMAN

Rocky and The Black Eye Mystery

SYLVIA SHERRY

JONATHAN CAPE
LONDON

For Mary Mulroy

First published 1992
Text © Sylvia Sherry 1992

Jonathan Cape Ltd, 20 Vauxhall Bridge Road, London SW1V 2SA

A CIP record for this book
is available from the British Library

ISBN 0-224-02721-2

Phototypeset by Intype, London
Printed and bound in Great Britain by
Butler & Tanner Limited, Frome and London

CHAPTER

1

Suzie Flanagan was crouched on the steps of Number 3, St Catherine's Square, her arms folded on her knees and her head resting on her arms. She'd been there an hour, ever since she came back from school, and hadn't moved.

There was nobody else in the Square, only Suzie, and the Square was becoming shadowy and cold. Suzie shivered.

Then there was a squeaking noise in the distance and Ellen-from-upstairs came through the Square, pushing the pram with her baby Trevor in it and a plastic bag of groceries on top of Trevor. She put the brake on the pram and shook back her long blonde hair.

"What yer sittin' der for, Suzie?" she asked.

Suzie did not move or say anything.

"Well, I'll have ter get past yer ter get in. Yer mind?"

Still Suzie did not move or say anything, and Ellen began to feel worried. She had lived upstairs to the Flanagans for some years, and she knew that Suzie, who was only seven, was a strange, silent girl and if she got upset was likely to take off and find a hiding place somewhere in the city and have everybody out searching for her.

"Yer mam not in?" she asked.

No answer.

"Yer not well, Suzie? Yer gorra pain some-where?"

Suzie muttered something that sounded like "Bad!"

"What's bad, but?" And getting no reply, "Rocky not around?" Then Ellen looked anxiously round the Square and at the ground floor of Number 3, where Suzie lived. There was no sign of anyone inside.

"Listen, Suzie," she said, "I'll go an' get Mr Oliver. Will yer keep an eye on Trevor an' me groceries?" But seeing that Suzie wasn't going to keep an eye on anything, she started running along the Square towards the house where Mr Oliver was caretaker. She hoped he'd be in the front garden, otherwise she'd have to ring the door-bell and maybe get Mrs Oliver who, in Ellen's opinion, was hard-faced.

But Mr Oliver was in the garden, putting a bit of paint on the front gate.

"Oh, Mr Oliver," Ellen cried, "Suzie's actin' queer an' she's locked out, an' I think she's goin' ter take off!"

Mr Oliver put down his paint brush.

"Come and see what I can do."

Mr Oliver squatted down beside Suzie. "Now den, Suzie," he said, "yer know me, don't yer, Suzie? Mr Oliver – der wingy – that's what Rocky calls me, in't it?" Mr Oliver had been a star player for Liverpool until he'd lost an arm in a car accident and became a wingy.

But he made no impression on Suzie, which was strange because she'd always trusted him.

"No idea wur her mam is?" he asked Ellen.

"Could be anywhere – maybe de housey."

"An' Rocky?"

Suzie shuddered again and muttered, "Want Rocky."

"*Wur's* he, but?" asked Ellen. "Should have been home by now. What'll we do?"

"Yer right, Ellen. She *will* take off. Can't risk leavin' her," said Mr Oliver. "I'll stay wid her."

Rocky was coming home from school the long way round by Larkspur Lane, partly because he knew Nabber Neville was going to be home and he might just be hanging about outside Pa Richardson's grocery in the hope that some of the Cats Gang would be there. He was right. The Nabber was leaning against the wire frames over Pa Richardson's windows, looking bored and chewing something – the Nabber was usually chewing something.

"Hi, Nabber!" he shouted. "How'd it go?"

The Nabber said nothing, only contemplated Chan's chippy opposite, and Rocky concluded that it hadn't gone well. The Nabber's mother had sent him for a week to a private boarding school where her cousin was a teacher, in the hope that the Nabber would take to it, leave the local comprehensive and so set himself on the track to becoming a yuppie, and get him out of the influence of boys like Rocky.

"Yer like it, well?" Rocky asked, also leaning against Pa Richardson's wire frames and contemplating Chan's chippy, while Pa Richardson peered anxiously out at *them*.

"Borin'," said the Nabber.

"Must of been posh, but?"

"Der was no carpets, just bare boards," said the Nabber, "an' the furniture was old stuff."

"Must of been just like *our* school," said Rocky.

"Der was bells goin' all the time an' then yer had ter go somewhere."

"Well, dat's just like . . ."

"An' yer had ter sleep in a dormitory – yer know like, wid lots of beds in it . . ." The Nabber's voice tailed off.

Rocky thought he was in shock, and he could understand it. After all, the Nabber's house had two bathrooms – the only house he knew like that – one upstairs that was there when they moved in and one downstairs that the Nabber's father had put in, but they couldn't use it because if you once turned on the water you couldn't get it off again without a major plumbing job that only the Nabber's father could do.

"Well," said Rocky, "yer don't have ter sleep in a dormitory at our school – yer can do it at yer desk. Dey never notice."

The Nabber resuscitated himself. "Had ter learn Latin," and he looked stern, as if he was going to draw a gun or make a speech.

"What's dat?"

"What der Romans spoke."

Rocky was lost. "Who's der Romans?"

"Never found out, but dey built a wall, an' yer'd think dey were der next-door neighbours, dey knew that much about dem. I learnt the names for a table in Latin – only thing I learnt. There's about six of them, all pretty much the same, an' the first one's *mensa*."

Rocky was astounded. "Yer mean dey had ter say six words for a table?"

"No." The Nabber stood up straight, recovering from his ordeal. "No, dey only used one of dem words, but I never figured out which."

For a few moments they contemplated the predicament of the Romans, then the Nabber asked, "Anythin' been movin' round here?"

"Been fairly busy," said Rocky. "Chick's Lot's keepin' low because dey flooded the market with a load of shoes from a warehouse dey done – dey was all left feet. Murky Evans's not a guest of de Queen any longer, and der's rumours of a new gang called the Bone-Breakers."

The Nabber yawned. "Nothin's changed," he said.

They started up the Steps that led to St Catherine's Square.

"Yer'll not be goin' back ter that place on a permanent basis? Yer mam won't force yer?"

"Dey won't have me back," said the Nabber. "I made certain. Dead borin'. Gorrany ideas for anythin'?" He sounded desperate.

"Sussin' a place out," said Rocky, though he wasn't.

"One of yer usual? Empty shop wid nothin' in it?"

"Listen, Nabber, when I suss a place . . ."

"I know. Always the same. We take the loot out, if there's any loot there, and then put it back. Typical! An' yer call yerself a genius!"

But Rocky did not respond. They were in St Catherine's Square, and the wingy shouted, "Rocky!" He saw that the wingy and Ellen were standing outside Number 3 and he started to run.

"Yer better see ter Suzie." Mr Oliver stood back.

"She's been sat der since I come back wid der shoppin'," said Ellen, "an' she won't say nothin'."

Rocky didn't like the look of things. He could see the tension in Suzie's crouched figure.

"Tatty-'ead, yer goin' ter move? Yer holdin' things up, sittin' der," he said cautiously.

Suzie shuddered again.

"Listen, Suzie, if yer don't move yerself . . ."

Suzie looked up at him. "Bad, Rocky," she said.

It *was* bad. There was blood on her mouth, her lower jaw was swollen, there was a big bruise on one side of her forehead and the eye beneath it was bloodshot.

Rocky pushed both hands furiously through his red hair, making it stand on end, and said fiercely but quite quietly because he didn't want to upset Suzie any more, "Who done it, Suzie? You tell me who done it to yer and I'll batter dem from here ter Birkenhead!"

Suzie just glared, then she held out her arm. There were knife cuts on it.

"Swine!" she said.

"Yer right there," said Mr Oliver, while Ellen tried to dab away the blood with her handkerchief. Suzie pulled away.

"Come on, Suzie. Yer have ter tell us who done it. Was it somebody at school?"

Suzie shook her head.

"Well – was it somebody like Mr Oliver? Well, somebody like me?"

Suzie kept on shaking her head.

"Wasn't me mam?" Rocky asked anxiously, because Suzie and her stepmother didn't get on.

Suzie shook her head, then pointed at Ellen-from-upstairs.

"Like her," she said.

Ellen's face went pink. "Me? What she mean, like me? I've never harmed her. I wuddent! What would I . . ."

"Doesn't mean *you*, Ellen," said Rocky. "Somebody *like* you."

"I've been accused, but," retorted Ellen.

"Yer have, luv," said the woman from Number 4, joining in. "Dat's libel. Yer could have dem for it."

"What's goin' on? Is der a fire? Have we been broke into?" It was Rocky's mother, Mrs Flanagan, looking quite wild.

"What'd we be broke into for, but? Nothin' ter take. It's Suzie, mam. Somebody's beat her up. Show her, Suzie."

Suzie looked up, scowling, held out her arm and muttered, "Swine."

"Who done that?" demanded Mrs Flanagan.

"We don't know – she was just sittin' there."

"She said it was me, but it wasn't. I wuddent!" put in Ellen-from-upstairs.

"Must have been when she was comin' back from school," said Rocky.

"That's right," agreed Ellen, with the air of someone who had cleared herself. "She was here when I come back from the shoppin' about four."

"An' *you* should have been here ter see ter her," added the woman from Number 4.

Mrs Flanagan bristled. "An' *you* should mind yer own business! An' get yerself away from my front window!"

"I'm on the pavement, an' that's public property!"

"Listen, mam," Rocky interrupted. "We've got

ter take Suzie down ter the scuffers in Larkspur Lane." He said it reluctantly. He preferred to avoid contact with the police – they'd pin something on you if they got the chance.

"Rocky's right. Have ter be reported," said Mr Oliver. "Has ter be investigated."

"Well, yer should know yer way," put in the woman from Number 4. "Yer've been there plenty, what with your Joey and *him*," meaning Rocky. She sniffed contemptuously. "Pity yer can't choose yer neighbours."

"Clear off, missus, or I'll put yer down a drain!" retorted Rocky. "Come on, mam. And give us yer hand, Suzie, and mind yer behave yerself."

"Well," said the Nabber, grinning as they passed him on their way to the Steps, "youse always put on a good show. See yer."

"Norrif I see yer first, yer won't," retorted Rocky, trying to persuade Suzie to stand up and walk and not to have to be dragged all the way to the cons' shop on her bottom.

"Not go, Rocky," she protested, shivering and near tears, which was unusual for Suzie. "Not go."

"Listen, tatty-'ead, I know how yer feel – it's the last place anybody ever wants ter go to. But it won't take long, see? An' when we get back, I'll buy yer somethin' at Pa Richardson's."

Suzie started walking then, her head down, the bow of ribbon in her hair limp. But she was thinking and said suddenly, "Ants. An' snakes."

"What yer on about?"

"Buy somethin' . . ."

"Said Pa Richardson's, not the zoo!"

12

The police station in Larkspur Lane was a red-brick building, not very large, and with its pointed-arched windows having the look of a small church or a run-down Sunday School that had somehow got itself lost between a Militant Tendency bookshop on one side and a butcher's shop on the other. Rocky had frequently run past it shouting insults through its open door, and he was further worried now when he noticed that a picture of a wanted man on the notice board, which he had personally and quite artistically altered to look like Constable McMahon complete with helmet, was still there.

Faced with the small crowd in the narrow passageway, led by an angry Mrs Flanagan, the desk sergeant wilted a little.

"Now then, Mrs Flanagan," he said, resigned. "What's ter do?"

"It's Suzie. She's been beat up. Look at her face! Lift yer face up will yer, Suzie!"

Reluctantly Suzie looked at the sergeant, frowning ferociously.

"Must of been when she was comin' back from school," said Rocky.

"That's right, because I just got back from the shoppin' an' she was on the step – and *I* didn't do it," Ellen put in, "whatever she says – an' *I've* always been very good to her! Especially when she was locked out!" Ellen and Mrs Flanagan exchanged angry looks.

The sergeant picked up the phone and said something quietly. In a few moments a woman police constable appeared.

"Suzie!" she said, seeing Suzie's face and arm. "Who did it?"

Suzie just glowered at her.

"Would you bring her through here, Mrs Flanagan, and we'll try to find out what happened."

"I'm comin' as well," said Rocky. "She'll not tell nothin' ter nobody except me."

"Well, *I'm* comin', 'cos I want ter know what she says," said Ellen.

"Only Mrs Flanagan and Suzie." The WPC was firm. "We'll get some tea . . ."

Mr Oliver, Ellen and Rocky sat down resignedly on a bench along the wall.

"She'll not tell nobody nothin'," Rocky reiterated and added "Scuffers!" loud enough for the sergeant to hear. But the sergeant was making another phone call.

Constable McMahon came in, supporting a man who was carrying a bunch of wilting flowers and a square box with B&Q printed on it. He looked very happy, if unsteady. Constable McMahon cast a practised eye over the three on the bench and Rocky heard him say to the sergeant, "Trouble again?"

"Yes! It is!" Rocky put in. "Somebody's mugged Suzie, an' maybe yer could put yer great intelligence inter findin' out *who*!"

"Now then, Rocky," said Mr Oliver. "He's naturally upset, Mac," he added to the constable.

"Store detective in B&Q caught this one at it," McMahon explained to the sergeant. "Think he's been merry-making. Can't get his name out of him, even."

"We'll see what's in his pockets . . ."

Just then a short, plump man carrying a case came in and went up to the desk.

"Medical practitioner," he announced to the sergeant. "Young girl, isn't it?"

"Dey done *you* as well, doc?" asked the man from B&Q with the flowers, in amazement.

The sergeant took the doctor into the room where Mrs Flanagan and Suzie were.

"Didn't know dey did doctors," said the man from B&Q.

"Here, Rocky," said the wingy, getting some money out of his pocket, "take this and get somethin' for Suzie when yer go home."

Rocky knew what to expect when the wingy gave him a handout – would be maybe forty or fifty pence.

"Thanks very much, Mr Oliver. Dat's great – make her that happy."

It made *him* happier, as well. Was a good skin, was Mr Oliver. "But," he added, "waste of time, dis. She'll not tell nobody nothin'."

The doctor and WPC reappeared and went into consultation with the sergeant. Rocky went over to them.

"What yer found out?" he demanded.

"Who's this boy?" asked the doctor.

"I'm Rocky O'Rourke. Suzie's my sister."

"Stepsister," put in the sergeant, adding confidentially, "The boy's father was lost at sea, and the mother married again."

"Yer can speak up – it's norra secret," Rocky said, though he hated having it talked about – had hated Flanagan, his stepfather, to begin with, though he turned out all right in the end. "What about Suzie?"

"I'm afraid your sister's been badly beaten up –

maybe for theft, or to frighten her for some reason?" The doctor looked thoughtful. "Must be a reason. She can go home, but if she's worse tomorrow, she should see your doctor. She's badly shocked and needs rest and quiet. Doesn't say much, does she?"

"Told dem she wouldn't. She never does. I'm the only one can get anythin' out of her – told youse, but youse wouldn't listen."

"And *did* you get anything out of her?" asked the sergeant.

"Only thing was . . ."

But Ellen interrupted. "I want clarifyin'," she said firmly. "It's my right."

The two policemen and the doctor looked startled.

"Yer want what, Ellen?" asked the sergeant.

"I've been accused, and I'm innercent. I wuddent of hurt her. I cuddent!"

"Hurt who, Ellen?" asked the WPC.

"Suzie. She said I mugged her, an' I didn't . . ."

"She didn't say *that*," said Rocky, exasperated. "She said *somebody like you* did it." He clutched his red hair and walked round shaking his head, giving a good impression of somebody being driven mental.

"So she does speak sometimes?" said the doctor.

"Well, yes, but this time – well, I made it like a game, see?" Rocky looked earnestly up at the three faces. "Asked her questions like did the one that mugged her *look like* me, or Mr Oliver, or Ellen . . ."

"He did. I can vouch for that," said Mr Oliver.

"An' she said *me*, an' it's lies an' I want . . ."
Ellen started up again.

"She didn't mean *you*, Ellen," said the sergeant.
"That's clear."

"Well." Ellen shook back her long blonde hair.
"That's somethin', anyway! An' I should think
so! It was said in front of witnesses – the woman
from Number 4 an' Mr Oliver an' . . ."

"I'll send in a report." The doctor hastily
pushed his way to the door as Suzie and Mrs
Flanagan appeared.

"Yer all right, tatty-'ead?" Rocky asked anxiously. Suzie looked very pale, with shiny patches
where ointment had been put on her bruises. The
bruise under one eye was swelling and blackening,
and her lips were swollen.

"I'll get whoever done this an' I'll *batter* dem!"
Rocky exclaimed.

"She needs a cup of hot, weak tea with plenty
of sugar and a warm bed," Ellen-from-upstairs
declared, and with a contemptuous look at Mrs
Flanagan added, "Not that she's likely to get it."

"You mind yer lip! I don't need advice from
you. I was bringin' up children when you was still
in nappies!" retorted Mrs Flanagan.

"Well, yer didn't make much of a job of it!"

"Ladies, please," the sergeant put in. "You can
go home now. Can you organize a peaceful
exodus, Dave?" he asked Mr Oliver, who nodded
and said, "Come on, Ellen. Give yer a hand up
the Steps with Trevor's pram. That's him yellin'
outside, in't it?"

Ellen swept out with another withering look at
Mrs Flanagan, who went red with anger and
grabbed Suzie's hand.

17

"Come on, *you*! The cheek of that girl! *And* I did her weddin' tea! – *and* she can't keep a man with her!"

Suzie pulled away and gripped the sleeve of Rocky's anorak. "Bad!" she said, frightened by the angry voices. "Bad!" in a kind of mumble, because of her swollen lips.

"Be all over by termorrer. Here, Suzie, yer can show me which lamp-post yer blacked yer eye on."

"Didn't!" shouted Suzie.

"Must of."

"Didn't!" And she began to sob.

Rocky put his arm round her. "Come on, tatty-'ead," he said.

The Flanagans had two rooms on the ground floor of Number 3. One was Rocky's bedroom, and his brother Joey's when he was home, and the other was a living-room. Coming into it in semi-darkness and then switching on the overhead light, it looked shabby and was cold. There was a bed along one wall which Mrs Flanagan shared with Suzie, a carpet with a hole in it, a table with a lumpy sofa behind it, a chair on each side of the electric fire and a gas cooker in a dark alcove, the ceiling above it festooned with cobwebs which Mrs Flanagan never remembered to get rid of. And there was an old alarm clock on the mantelpiece that gave out regular, disturbing noises.

Mrs Flanagan switched on the electric fire, sat down in her chair and kicked off her shoes. Suzie stood by herself, saying nothing, glowering and shivering.

Rocky pulled the curtains together over the

window and fastened them together with the safety pin, because they didn't close properly. He switched on the television, and the room looked a lot better.

"Suzie should be in bed, mam," he said.

"Well, get her into it," said Mrs Flanagan, "an' put the kettle on. I don't know," she added, "why I ever married Flanagan and took *her* on," meaning Suzie. "She's nothin' but trouble, an' *he's* never here – and he's given up sendin' any money. An' as for her-upstairs, I'll never open my mouth to her again! The cheek!"

Suzie went on shivering and glowering at her stepmother.

"Come on, tatty-'ead," said Rocky, "get yerself down in front of the fire, an' I'll get yer somethin'. What's der ter eat, mam?"

Mrs Flanagan looked distracted. "I don't know! Der'll be somethin'. Have a look. I can't get on wid things wid all this goin' on." Then, having considered, she added, "There's a big tin of beans an' a loaf. Just got dem yesterday."

Rocky made some tea and some beans on toast, wishing that his father was still alive or that Flanagan would come home, and worrying about Suzie and how he was going to find out who had beaten her up. Suzie sat on the floor eating, and so did Rocky, watching the television in a trance until Suzie dropped her plate and fell over, asleep, on the carpet.

They were both sleeping, Suzie and his mother. Rocky pulled on his anorak and went out.

CHAPTER

2

Especially at night St Catherine's Square, if you were standing outside Number 3, was like a deep, dark canyon with the tall terraced houses on three sides and St Catherine's Buildings on the fourth, lighted windows puncturing its sides like portholes on a big liner. Towards the River Mersey the huge square tower of the Anglican Cathedral stood out against a blue-black sky with a white moon in it, like a big head on big shoulders, watching him. The street lights didn't make much difference to the Square – they were only small beacons in the darkness, and on the patch of trodden ground that had once been a garden the abandoned car and the builder's hut were dark hulks. A vicious little breeze from the river rustled discarded newspapers round his feet and lifted an empty take-away tray backwards and forwards.

It didn't depress Rocky, in fact it made him feel better, because he loved the city at night – the light and darkness, the shouts and the sound of breaking bottles, the noise of traffic, the feeling of danger. Was an adventure, something to make you sweat. Was all right. And he *would* find out who beat up Suzie. Maybe his Gang, the Cats, would be down on Larkspur Lane. He pulled his anorak up round his ears, leapt on to the low wall around the abandoned garden, balanced along its slippery surface and jumped off at the top of the Steps that led down to Larkspur Lane.

It was just as he was about to run down the Steps that he was grabbed from behind, his arm twisted up against his back. A voice said, "Wur's he? Your Joey?"

Rocky froze. He recognized the voice.

"Spain," he said. "In Spain. An' will yer let go . . ."

"When's he back?"

"Not comin' back!"

"Heard different. An' you listen. When he comes back tell him Murky Evans an' the Crown Street Gang'll, be after him. He owes us. An' I've gorra knife ready for him. Got it?"

"Haven't gorra holler head! Now gerroff!"

"Right!"

Rocky's arm was released and Murky Evans plodded away towards Princes Boulevard – he always plodded, did Murky. Rocky fell backwards against the wall, trying to move his arm, which was painful. He was shaking. But he was suddenly angry and shouted, "An' you watch out, Murky Evans, because *I'll* do *you!*"

There was a gruff sort of laugh from the direction in which Murky had disappeared. But Rocky was worried. The Crown Street Gang were ruthless – and why did Murky Evans think Joey was coming home? Must have some information.

"Hi, Rocky!"

It was Beady Martin coming out into the Square, hunching his shoulders against the cold wind. "Goin' down the Lane. Yer comin'?"

"Was goin'."

Beady thought Rocky sounded a bit strange.

"What's it, Rocky?" he asked. "Is it Suzie? Me mam heard about her."

"Was Murky Evans. He got me – just now. Twisted me arm. Not broke it, but."

That worried Beady. "Murky Evans? What's he got on yer?"

"Not me. Our Joey."

Outlined against the light from the window of Chan's chippy in Larkspur Lane were two figures: the Nabber wearing an American baseball cap, and Billy Griffiths sitting on his tricycle, a scarf wrapped round his neck, frowning down at the handle-bars of his trike. Billy was disabled and could only get around easily on his tricycle. They weren't saying much to each other, the Nabber and Billy, but then they never did, not liking each other. Little Chan wasn't there.

"Hi." Rocky leant back against the window of Chan's chippy and said nothing more.

"All right, Rocky?" asked Billy, sensing that it wasn't. "Heard about Suzie. How's she?"

"Bit of a mess."

"Who would have done it, but?" asked Beady. "Think about it. She wasn't carryin' money, was she? Wasn't fightin' nobody, was she?"

"Could have thrown a half brick at somebody," said the Nabber, knowing Suzie's habits.

"She wouldn't do that without provocation," said Billy.

"Dat's a big word," said the Nabber sarcastically. "Wur'd yer get it from?"

"An' youse is as big a mistake as the Post Office tower that's stopped revolvin' an' just as useless," said Rocky. "Don't know who done it. But I'll find out."

"Rocky the Susser," said the Nabber. "Can suss anybody out."

"Listen, Nabber," said Rocky fiercely, "got news for yer. Murky Evans just tried to do me on the Steps."

"He did," confirmed Beady.

That worried the Nabber. "What's he got on yer?"

"Not me. Our Joey. But he could come back to us."

"About the Ratman?"

"The Ratman."

For a few moments they were silent, remembering the Ratman. Then Rocky said, "Got forty pence from der wingy terday ter get Suzie some sweets. Get some chips wid it. Make it up to her."

Unexpectedly, the Nabber got some money out of his pocket. "Yer can use this as well an' get some mushy peas," he said generously. It brightened them all up and they went into Chan's chippy.

Mr Chan, who was frying, gave them a quick glance over his shoulder, and Mrs Chan looked at them briefly as she wrapped up an order. They got in the queue and when they reached the counter Rocky asked, "Little Chan in?"

"He is doing his homework, which is what you should be doing," said Mrs Chan sternly.

"We've done it, but," said Rocky cheekily, putting their money on the counter. "Can we have chips an' mushy peas an' salt an' vinegar for dat?"

Mrs Chan did not reply but picked up the money and began to put up the chips and mushy peas. She did not approve of Rocky and the Cats Gang.

Outside the chippy they shared the chips and mushy peas with the help of the plastic forks Rocky had thoughtfully picked up.

They were quite relaxed until the Nabber, who had been very thoughtful, screwed up his chip paper and dropped it on the pavement.

"What would Murky Evans be after us for?" he asked.

"Wants ter know when Joey's back from Spain, because Joey took the Ratman's money when Murky had planned on gettin' it," said Rocky.

"Well," said the Nabber reasonably, "Murky's got nothin' ter complain about, has he? Him and Joey wasn't the only ones after the Ratman's money. I seem ter remember *we* was the ones sussin' der place for hours an' gettin' inside der house wid der rats runnin' round and findin' that drawer full of money an' leavin' a window open so we could get back in. And what happened? The Ratman was dead an' the money gone. Brilliant effort that was, planned by our great hero, Rocky the Susser. Best of yer famous failures! Joey gets the money an' we get Murky after *us*."

"Wasn't a failure," Billy protested. "Was an accident. Joey saw the window was open."

"That's right, Billy. An' I'll do yer, Nabber Neville, if yer don't put a trap on yer moey. An' *I* was the first inter dat house, an' we could of got the money if our Joey hadn't got it. Anyway, Murky Evans was after it as well, an' he's after our Joey for it. An' when did *you* plan anythin', Nabber? Apart from escapin' from dat school yer

24

didn't like, an' dat took yer a week! Could of got meself out of Walton Jail quicker!"

"Or Risley," added Beady.

"Dat's right – or Risley!"

There was a pause, then the Nabber said ominously, "Yer right, but. If he's after Joey he won't leave *us* out, Murky. There's the family connection. If yer get involved with the O'Rourkes, it'll pay yer ter take out insurance."

"Belt up or I'll put yer eye in a sling!"

"Not Rocky's fault!" said Beady. "Was doin' his best."

They had all got heated up over the issue, and their voices were loud enough to attract the attention of the customers in Chan's chippy, and of Mr and Mrs Chan as well. Even Little Chan could be seen looking anxiously over the counter.

"You lot got no homes to go to?" asked a voice. It was Constable McMahon, accompanied by a WPC.

"Got his mam wid him," muttered Rocky.

"Don't think Mrs Chan wants you hanging around the shop, not unless yer plannin' ter buy. Yer not? Well then . . ."

Billy, Beady and the Nabber looked uneasy and inclined to go, but Rocky retorted, "It's a free country, in't it? An' we've bought!"

"So that's where the litter's come from. Suzie said anything, Rocky?"

"No. She's asleep."

"So's his mam," muttered the Nabber.

"Well, if she does say anything or you get any ideas . . . And by the way, we're interested in information about an artist who did a good job on a WANTED notice outside the police station."

25

"Gorra lot of dem round here – artists," said Rocky. "Come on, Gang."

"Before you go, pick up those chip papers and put them somewhere where they can't blow about." And Constable McMahon and the WPC left.

When they had gone Rocky, to the surprise of the Cats, dutifully picked up the discarded chip papers and carefully put them under the wind-screen wipers of a parked car.

"Won't blow away now," he commented. As they moved on he said, "Could be Murky Evans did Suzie. Could think she might know somethin' about Joey."

"But what me mam heard," said Beady, "was that it was somebody like Ellen did it."

"Somehow," said the Nabber thoughtfully, "I can't see how Murky could have done himself up ter look like Ellen. Not without major surgery."

"Murky could have got a girl lookin' like Ellen ter frighten Suzie, but," said Billy.

"But it's a well-known fact round here," said the Nabber, "that Suzie never says anythin' ter nobody."

This was true, but it annoyed Rocky that the Nabber was doing the thinking and he grabbed the Nabber's baseball cap, shouting, "Catch!" and threw it to Billy who caught it and threw it to Beady who threw it to Rocky. The Nabber shouted, "My dad'll do youse – *he* got that hat for me!"

"Thought I just told you lot to go home," said Constable McMahon, returning unexpectedly, "but if you want taking in on a disorderly behaviour . . ."

Billy disappeared in the direction of St Catherine's Buildings and Rocky, Beady and the Nabber (having retrieved his baseball hat) ran up the Steps. There was no sign of Murky.

"Could be, but," panted Rocky. "Could be Murky Evans organized Suzie's mugging. Could be. Wouldn't put nothin' past him."

CHAPTER
3

Rocky had a restless night with Murky Evans plodding through his dreams. Next morning he woke up, jerked out of sleep by the memory that Suzie had been hurt and that he had to see how she was. He wandered into the next room and was shaken into total consciousness. His mother was already up, dressed in her best green suit, and was combing through her black curls in front of the small mirror on the mantelpiece. The curtains were still closed and the light on, and Suzie was a small bundle in the bed. It was as though he'd got into a time warp, and he was bewildered. According to the old alarm clock on the mantelpiece he wasn't late for school. In fact he was early; but what had got his mother up at this time and given her the urge to get herself dressed up?

"What yer doin', mam?" he asked. "The Queen comin'?"

"I'm goin' ter yer Auntie Chrissie's," said Mrs Flanagan firmly, still working on her curls.

"But it's – it's not light yet, an' what yer goin' ter me Auntie Chrissie's for?"

"Dat's my business. An' *you'll* have ter stay in an' look after *her*." She jabbed her comb in the direction of Suzie.

Rocky considered the implications of this. "Yer mean yer tellin' me ter sag school?"

"I'm tellin' yer yer stayin' here."

Rocky sat down on the lumpy sofa. It was a new situation to be ordered to sag school instead of deciding to do it himself.

"I'll have ter have a note for termorrer, but," he said. "Ter explain. But dat'll make it official if it's comin' from you." He began to contemplate the possible activities of a free day. Maybe the Nabber would sag as well and they could go downtown. "Right," he said. "Great."

"Yer not havin' a picnic," said Mrs Flanagan. "Yer stayin' here wid *her* to see nothin' happens. I don't want the social worker round sayin' she's neglected. If they take her away, Flanagan'll clear off. Not that he needs any encouragement," she added to herself, and put on some lipstick.

"But, mam, I can't! Can't just stay in here all day! What'll I do?"

"Yer've got the telly and yer've got her ter keep an eye on and that should do. An' *you* make sure she doesn't go ruinin' my books." This was a reference to Mrs Flanagan's valuable collection of paper-backed romances which were stacked on a stool at the end of the bed and which Suzie, depending on her feelings towards Mrs Flanagan, was inclined to scribble over or shred.

Rocky became increasingly desperate as the implications of a day in the flat with Suzie became clearer. "Hi, but listen," he said. "What we goin' ter eat? Der's nothin' in. We had the beans last night."

"Here." Mrs Flanagan thrust a five-pound note at him. "Get what yer want wid dat. An' I'll want der change."

Rocky was stunned. Then he said, "But if I go

out ter get somethin' ter eat, I have ter leave Suzie."

"Yer'll not be away a fortnight just down ter Pa Richardson's, will yer?"

"What's it all about, but? What yer goin' off for?"

"I've had a shock," said Mrs Flanagan, and picked up her handbag.

"What shock?"

"Never you mind," said Mrs Flanagan grimly.

"Hi, mam!"

"What's it?"

"Der key. Haven't gorra key! Can't find mine."

Mrs Flanagan hesitated, then reluctantly she gave Rocky her door key. "An' mind yer in when I get back."

"When'll dat be, but?"

There was no answer. The door was slammed. Rocky sat down in front of the electric fire to get warm. What was the shock his mam had had? This time in the morning?

He considered things. Suzie was still dead out. He'd have to leave her to get some food – and what could he do all day in the flat? He buttered a slice of bread and tried to work things out.

Half an hour later he was knocking on the door of Ellen-from-upstairs' flat. She came out in her dressing gown with Trevor, who had orange juice dribbling down his chin, in her arms.

"What's it, Rocky?" asked Ellen cautiously.

"Listen, Ellen, it's me mam. She's gone off for the day and left me wid Suzie."

"Well, I'm sorry, Rocky, but I can't take on the responsibility – not wid Suzie. She's had a bad time an' she's not well, an' yer never know what she'll get up to next. I'm not takin' on the responsibility."

"Ellen," Rocky pleaded, "can yer just listen for her for a half hour so I can go down ter Pa Richardson's for some things?"

"Well, I could do that. But I don't really like her bein' left by herself. Tell yer what, Rocky, yer could tell me when yer goin' an' I could come down an' sit wid Suzie – just till yer back, mind. I'm not sittin' der for hours. An' I did make me mind up I wuddent set foot in your place again, not after yer mam . . ."

"I know dat, Ellen, an' thanks very much. Yer a good skin. I'll get meself ready."

"Wur's she gone, but, yer mam?"

"Me Auntie Chrissie's."

"What for, but?"

"Says she's had a shock."

"I'd give her a shock," said Ellen, quite viciously for Ellen.

"But she did do yer wedding tea," said Rocky desperately.

"I never want ter hear about dat again," said Ellen. "Suzie had her breakfast?"

"Not yet. Der's some bread an' butter . . ."

"You make sure ter give me the key when yer go ter Pa Richardson's an' I'll go down straight away an' give Suzie somethin' ter eat. All right?"

"Thanks, Ellen."

Rocky had hoped for more, but you had to take what you could get. He was starting down the stairs when Ellen remarked, "Saw yer mam go out. Ter yer Auntie Chrissie's. All dressed up, wasn't she? Always is when she goes ter yer

31

Auntie Chrissie's. Yer Auntie Chrissie ever come here?"

"No."

"Ever seen her?"

Rocky was puzzled by this questioning. "Well, no."

"Sure it's not yer Uncle Chris?" And Ellen shut the door.

Rocky was stunned by this suggestion, but as he went downstairs he thought Ellen might be on to something. Could be his mam had another Flanagan in the background. For emergencies. Could be. Could be a better Flanagan than the current one, who was probably not coming back anyway. Was interesting. And the next one might have more money. As he considered the possibilities, he got dressed, switched off the electric fire, concealed his mother's paper-backed romances in the cupboard, had another look at Suzie, got a plastic carrier bag, the five-pound note and the key and went upstairs to Ellen.

The Cats were hanging about outside Pa Richardson's. The Nabber was staring gloomily through the shop window with its wire grid, and Pa Richardson was watching him nervously. Billy was on his trike and Beady and Little Chan were comparing notes on their separate productions of the previous day's homework. They looked round as Rocky came running towards them, plastic carrier over his arm.

"Hi!" he shouted."Hi, listen!"

"Out early ter do yer shoppin'?" commented the Nabber sarcastically. "Proper little housewife, in't he?"

"I'll do you, Nabber Neville! I'll batter yer round der Square yet! Me mam's gone off an' I'm saggin' school." He did not at that point fill in the picture.

"Yer saggin'?" The Nabber was interested.

"Yes. Yer on?"

"Downtown?"

"Dat's right. Just get some things first. What about youse?" he asked the rest of the Cats hopefully.

But the others were reluctant, not to say definitely against it, and they drifted off along Larkspur Lane.

"Right," said the Nabber. "Downtown."

"Well, I just have to – it's a bit . . ."

"Spaniard in der works?" The Nabber was suspicious.

"Well, yer see, me mam's gone off for ter day an' I have ter see ter Suzie, but I thought, Nabber, yer could come ter our place an' we could watch some telly, an' I've got enough for fish an' chips . . ."

The Nabber yawned. "Dead borin'," he said. "I've never had an ambition ter be a child-minder. See yer."

"But Nabber . . ."

The Nabber only walked on, waving a farewell as he went. And then shouted, "If yer free of yer nanny duties, lunch-time I'll be at der school gates."

Rocky was furious. Get you for that, Nabber Neville, he thought, and pushed open the door of Pa Richardson's shop. Without thinking of the impression he was making, he glared round angrily.

Pa Richardson and the early shopper he was serving looked at him nervously.

"That's two eighty, Mrs Harrison, so that's twenty change," said Pa Richardson. Mrs Harrison left hurriedly and Pa Richardson, looking like a underfed bumble bee, asked Rocky, "Yer wantin' (sniff) somethin'?"

"Wouldn't have come in if I didn't want somethin', would I?" answered Rocky.

"Got any (sniff) idea what yer want?"

Rocky considered what he wanted and what he might nick. "Think I'll have some corned beef," he said, dog-butties in mind, "an' three of dem small pizzas, an' have yer got any pies?"

"How much (sniff) corned beef?"

"Quarter pound. An' a tin of peas – big one."

"Marrowfat or . . . ?"

"Marrowfat, an' three slices of ham cut thin. An' what's these cakes goin' for?"

"What they're always goin' for – forty pence each."

"Rip off!"

"Yer don't (sniff) have to buy them. Hear that sister of yours s'been in trouble (sniff)."

"Can call it dat. Somebody beat her up."

Pa Richardson placed a tin of marrowfat peas on the counter and said thoughtfully, "Beat her (sniff) up?" Then he put his hands on the counter and stared at Rocky. "Yer don't mean it?"

"She's been punched up an' cut," said Rocky.

Pa Richardson sniffed several times and then said, "It's disgustin'. Is she gettin' over it? Is she in der hospital? I mean, I always had ter watch her here wid her hands on the sweets, but muggin' . . ."

34

"She'll be all right, Mr Richardson," said Rocky, seeing a possible advantage in Pa Richardson's concern. "She'll gerrover it."

"Give yer somethin' for her," said Pa Richardson, and he turned his back to look over his jars of sweets and boxes of chocolates. Rocky took the opportunity to pick up two cakes and put them in his plastic carrier.

"Now yer sister. What'd she like?"

"Beastly Wobblies an' snakes an' white mice an' false teeth, but yer don't have ter *give* dem to us, because I got forty pence from Mr Oliver for her."

"Well, you pick forty penceworth of Beastly Wobblies an' der rest (sniff) an' give her this." Pa Richardson carefully placed a half pound box of chocolates on the counter and added a tube of Smarties.

Rocky was overcome by this generosity, but then a woman who had come into the shop without his noticing said, "He's nicked two of yer cakes, Mr Richardson."

"Haven't!" shouted Rocky indignantly.

"Yer have. I knew it, but yer can have dem free, seeing Suzie's been mugged," said Pa Richardson.

"Yer don't need to . . ."

"I want to (sniff). An' yer might tell yer pals ter stop (sniff) leanin' on my wire frames."

"Tell dem," said Rocky. "An' thanks, Mr Richardson. Yer a good skin."

"Doin' it for Suzie. Not be a minute, missus," Pa Richardson said to the other customer. "Just reckon this lot up. Yer can (sniff) pay for it?" he added anxiously to Rocky.

Rocky produced his five-pound note. "Dat do yer?"

CHAPTER

4

The Lane was deserted when Rocky came out of Pa Richardson's, and the day stretched ahead of him with no excitement and nothing to do except look after Suzie. Get some comics out of the fiver, he thought, and he started towards the newsagents, only stopping to look at the shop next to Pa Richardson's, which had shown no sign of life for years, its window displaying only dead flies, sun-faded blankets, baby clothes and a notice saying "Join our Xmas Club" and another saying "Under New Manijment". But now the door was open, the windows empty, the sound of hammering was coming from inside and there was a view of several workmen. It had never been a place worth doing before, because you couldn't do much with dead flies and old blankets and baby clothes, but it could be promising in the future, he thought. Would suss it.

Going into the newsagents, he saw that they still had a notice on the door asking for "paper deliverers", and that had been there some time. Must be a shortage, he concluded, and considered the possibilities. Would depend on what they paid, because he could do with some money coming in, and he could buy things for Suzie. But his mam wouldn't have to know about it, because she'd want a cut.

The man at the post office counter looked at him over his half-moon spectacles and his plump wife straightened papers on the counter and smiled. Rocky smiled back, having something in mind.

"Just gerrin' me comic," he said, and went to look at the shelves, knowing what he wanted but taking time to think. He would get the *Eagle* and also the *Dandy*, because Suzie was interested in the activities of Dinah Mo, but usually he cut the cost by slipping the *Dandy* inside the *Eagle* and paying for only one. On this occasion he thought it would pay off to be honest.

"Have dese two," he said to the woman, with as honest a smile as he could manage, as he paid up the full amount. "Yer still wantin' somebody ter do the papers?"

"We are."

"Well, I want ter put in for it, an' I'll take the job on."

"Haven't been offered it yet, have you?" asked the man with the granny bicycles on his nose.

"No," said Rocky angrily, "but I'm offerin' to do it. Would get yer out of a difficulty. An' what's der pay?"

"What's your name?" asked the woman. "I've seen you around but . . ."

"I'm Rocky O'Rourke. Live in St Catherine's Square. Yer can ask anybody. So that's on, is it? Except for der pay?"

"No, it's not," said the woman. "Two things we need. One, your parents' consent, and two, somebody who'll guarantee that you're honest, reliable and a good time-keeper."

"Well, me mam . . ."

"Can't be yer mam. Has ter be somebody objective."

Rocky thought about it. "Right," he said. "Get somebody. What yer payin'?"

"Five pounds a week for twenty drops."

Didn't sound bad. Worth paying for the extra comic if he got the job.

"See yer," and he went along Larkspur Lane reading his comic and wondering who would speak objectively about him. The Nabber certainly wouldn't. And he couldn't trust McMahon. There was the superintendent of the Baptist Youth Club, but they seemed to change every six months, and he hadn't been there for a year, nearly. But there was Mr Oliver. He might do it, especially knowing the family's circumstances, including Suzie's mugging. But maybe he knew *too much* about him, the wingy. Pity he wasn't Enok, the Doomlord's son in the *Eagle*, because he could have been warped into someone objective and done his own recommending.

In Number 3, Ellen-from-upstairs was in front of the electric fire, Trevor was sitting on the hole in the carpet, rattling a tin with some dried peas in it, and Suzie was up, having some cereal and milk. Her face was still swollen and her eye black. She squinted up at him.

"All right, tatty-'ead?"

Suzie nodded. She was still dazed.

"Yer've taken yer time, Rocky," said Ellen.

"Sorry, Ellen, but yer know like . . ."

"Well, I'll gerroff," said Ellen. "Yer'll let me have me plate back when Suzie's finished? Yer mam wouldn't like me puttin' me nose inter things. She should be here, yer know like, Rocky. She shouldn't of left Suzie." And she picked up Trevor.

"Know dat. An' thanks, Ellen." Rocky fended off the spoon Trevor was waving in his face. "See what I've got for Suzie. Here, tatty-'ead, finish yer scoff, an' here's yer comic an' yer Beastly Wobblies an' false teeth an' white mice – dey're all from Mr Oliver. An' a box of chocolates and some Smarties from Pa Richardson."

"Wouldn't let her eat all that lot of sweets at one go. Make her sick." Ellen departed and the flat was suddenly quiet and felt empty.

"Here, Suzie," said Rocky, "yer can have dis red biro ter colour some pictures in wid." And he turned on the television.

Suzie was stunned by the gifts, but she was soon into the white mice and scribbling with the biro. By the time Rocky had read his comic, watched some telly and made some dog-butties with the corned beef, he was getting desperate. He went to examine Suzie's attempts at art just to take his mind off the boredom. Suzie had given up colouring and had found a piece of paper and drawn a house which had a definite lean to it, with a woman at the door, scowling and with her arms stretched out and long fingers to her hands.

"Bad, Rocky," said Suzie.

"Agree wid yer, Suzie," said Rocky. "Yer'll not make it in der paint business."

"This, Rocky," Suzie said urgently, pointing to another drawing she'd done of a long oblong with a round thing stuck on one end. "Good."

"Yer right," he said, but he was thinking that he hoped the mugging hadn't affected her brain.

There was no sign of his mam. Better to be in school, he thought. I can't stay here for the rest of the day.

"Tatty-'ead," he said, "yer can walk, can't yer?"

Suzie nodded, her mouth full of dog-butty.

"Yer want ter go out?"

Suzie nodded again.

"Wur to, but?"

"Prinney Park," Suzie spluttered through the dog butty.

"Don't think I could stand the excitement," said Rocky. "Mind, wid your eye we could be a sensation. Come on, finish yer butty. See if we can find Mr Oliver, an' yer can thank him for the beastlies."

Mr Oliver was on the doorstep of Number 3.

"Hello der, Rocky. Just comin' to ask how Suzie was. She looks a mess. Yer not takin' her out? An' why yer not at school?"

"S'like this, Mr Oliver," Rocky said, with his mind on what he wanted to work up to. "Me mam had to go ter me Auntie Chrissie's, so I had ter stay an' see ter Suzie. But I thought she should have a bit of a walk an' some fresh air."

Mr Oliver considered the situation.

"Yer mam shouldn't have gone, but," he said. "She should be here."

"She says she's had a shock."

"We all have those. Doesn't mean we clear off an' . . ."

"S'all right, Mr Oliver. I've given her a dog-butty, an' me mam's givin me a note for der school."

"It's still not right! I'd ask yer inter my place, Rocky, but yer know what the wife's like."

41

"I do, Mr Oliver. An' Suzie wants ter thank yer for the Beastly Wobblies an' false teeth. Go on, Suzie."

For some reason Suzie only frowned and said, "Bad! Swine!"

"Sorry, Mr Oliver," said Rocky apologetically. "She's not over it yet."

"Not surprisin'. If she's no better tomorrow, she should see the doctor. An' what are the Cats doin' about footy this season? I've heard nothin' from youse. Should start with a practice in Prinney Park Saturday."

"I'll have a word wid . . ."

"Yer'll not have a word wid. *You're* the captain?"

"Dat's right."

"Well, get on wid it and let me know. Ten o'clock if yer can get yer act tergether."

"See to it. Really." Rocky took a deep breath. "Mr Oliver, was goin' ter ask yer somethin'."

"What's it?"

"Well, the shop on Larkspur Lane wants somebody ter deliver papers."

"Seen der notice."

"Well, I asked about it. An' dey said I had ter have somebody to speak for me."

"Yer want the job? S'not easy, yer know, gettin' up early an' goin' round in the dark. Could be dangerous."

"Dat's nothin'. Just dat somebody has ter tell them I'm honest, reliable an' a good time-keeper."

Mr Oliver stared at him, then he took a short walk along the Square and came back.

"What yer want der job for ?"

"For der money."

"Dat's honest," said Mr Oliver. "Yer reliable in lookin' after Suzie, an' if yer get the Cats' team inter Prinney Park at ten on Saturday, yer a good timekeeper, and *then* I'll have a word with the shop in Larkspur Lane."

"But, Mr Oliver . . ."

"Get *on* wid it, Rocky. See yer on Saturday."

There weren't a lot of people in the park, which was not surprising since it looked as though it had been abandoned, with the grass all patches, the lake drying up and mainly a dump for dustbins, supermarket trolleys, newspapers and empty Coke cans – even the ducks had departed. In the shelter beside the lake two young boys were loosening the one remaining bench from the wall, presumably with the intention of taking it away and selling it. The only other sign of life was a man on a tractor who seemed to be employed to drive it round at intervals.

"Who done it to yer? Wish yer could tell me," said Rocky.

Suzie only frowned.

"Look, Suzie . . ."

"Swine! Swine! Swine!" shouted Suzie, and picking up a large stone prepared to throw it at a passing dog-walker.

"Will yer drop it, Suzie!" shouted Rocky. "Yer'll have us taken inter custody!"

Suzie dropped the stone. "Bad, Rocky," she said.

"Know dat, tatty-'ead. Come on. Be gettin' dark soon. We'll go back home. See if me mam's back."

Mrs Flanagan was back. She was standing outside Number 3 Catherine's Square looking frantic. When she saw Rocky and Suzie, she shouted,

"Wur've yer been? Yer left me locked out an' I've been waitin'!"

Ellen-from-upstairs pushed up her window and remarked, "Well, now yer know what it's like!"

"You shurrup and mind yer own business!"

"Well, you mind yours den!" And Ellen shut the window.

"The cheek!" said Mrs Flanagan. "Get yerselves in."

But Suzie pulled back, glaring at Mrs Flanagan. "Not go, Rocky," she said. "Not go in."

"Yer have to, tatty-'ead. An' it'll be all right. Yer've not done nothin' wrong. Come on."

"Wur's de key?" demanded Mrs Flanagan.

"Lost it," said Rocky.

"Lost it?"

"In Prinney Park lake."

Mrs Flanagan was speechless for a few moments. Then, "Yer *lost* it? Yer *lost* it? Well, yer'd better get back inter dat lake an' find it, or we'll have no place ter go except ter the Salvation Army hostel!"

"S'all right, mam," said Rocky grinning. "Just found it. In me pocket."

Mrs Flanagan took the key and gave Rocky a slap round the face in return. They all went into Number 3 in an unhappy mood.

Mrs Flanagan sat down in her chair in front of the electric fire without switching it on or kicking off her shoes. Suzie got behind the sofa and stood there stiffly, watching, afraid there might be a fight. Rocky dropped on to the sofa, very worried. He hadn't seen his mother like this before, only when she had her intuitions.

"What's it, mam?" he asked cautiously. "Auntie Chrissie not well, like?"

"Auntie Chrissie!" said Mrs Flanagan, scornfully.

"Well, what's it?"

Mrs Flanagan took a few moments to think before she took a piece of paper out of her handbag. "Have a look at this," she said. "Been worryin' me all day. Was der shock. Was pushed under the door this morning."

Rocky straightened out the crumpled piece of paper. On it was written in capitals, "WEN JOEY COMES BACK WE DO HIM."

"What's it mean, Rocky? Joey's not comin' back. I mean, he's doin' all right in Spain, an' he had all that money from his job. An' what's dis lot to do wid him?"

"Crown Street Gang. Murky Evans runs dem. He got on ter me. Dey're goin' ter do Joey if he comes back."

"Do Joey? What for, but? What's them got ter do wid Joey?"

"Joey stole some money when Murky Evans was plannin' ter get it." Rocky didn't explain that *he* had been the first one with the idea of getting the money. Only confuse his mother if you complicated things.

"Joey!" Mrs Flanagan was indignant. "Joey never stole nothin'!"

"Steal a bit of fish off a cat, Joey would."

"Yer a liar! Joey's a..."

Rocky stopped listening to what Joey was – good son, among other things. But he knew what Joey was – a cheap crook who stole from his mother. 'Steal from your mother and your hand'll drop off.' Hadn't happened with Joey, but. Battered Flanagan as well. But Murky Evans *must* have had a tip-off that Joey was coming back. Joey must have gone through the Ratman's money.

At that moment Suzie started to scream. Mrs Flanagan shot out of her chair.

"Stop that! Stop her, or I'll batter her!" she shouted.

"Give it up, Suzie!" shouted Rocky. "Give it up! He's not comin' back, Joey. Yer needn't worry. Here, have another Beastly Wobbly and shurrup!"

Suzie put the Beastly Wobbly into her mouth and began to cry.

"Come on, Suzie. He's not comin' back, Joey. He's not comin'."

"Sore," Suzie sobbed. "Sore." She rubbed her eye.

"Well, don't do dat, or it'll be sorer. Yer'd be better in bed, tatty-'ead."

"Yes. Get her inter Joey's bed. I've had enough of her," said Mrs Flanagan, switching on the fire and kicking off her shoes. "Should take dis note ter the police," she added reflectively.

"Wouldn't do dat, mam," said Rocky quickly. "Yer'll have der scuffers on ter Joey. An' yer only givin' dem a job ter help wid the promotion. Tatty-'ead, yer'll have some tea an' a pizza and gerroff ter bed. All right?"

Suzie looked at him and smiled for the first time since she'd been mugged. "Have pizza, go ter bed," she said.

"That's right. Yer want a pizza as well, mam?"

Mrs Flanagan gave the suggestion some thought. "Well, better have somethin'. Had nothin' all day."

"Did me Auntie Chrissie not . . . ?"

"I'm not discussin' yer Auntie Chrissie again. Don't want ter say nothin' about her."

"Well, I don't know nothin' . . ."

"Good, Rocky," said Suzie.

"What's good, Suzie? Yer haven't got yer pizza yet. Yer puttin' dem on, mam?"

"Good, Rocky. Old woman. Good."

"What yer on about, tatty-'ead?" Rocky started to heat up the pizzas since his mother was engrossed in re-reading Murky Evans's note and had obviously given up everything. I'm going to school tomorrow, he decided. I'll go early. It's easier than all this.

"Woman in box," said Suzie. "Good, Rocky. Help."

Rocky pushed his hands through his red hair in desperation. "Listen, tatty-'ead, yer must be sufferin' from shock still. Get yerself inter bed an' I'll bring yer a pizza."

Wish me dad was here, he thought. Wish Flanagan even was here. Then he thought that tomorrow he would take another look at the shop they were doing up next to Pa Richardson's, and since his mam was providing a note for one day's sag anyway, he could probably organize it to cover tomorrow as well and go downtown with the Nabber. Joey wouldn't come back, he thought. Wouldn't take the risk. Then he wondered whether Joey knew what the risk was.

He thought about the paper round and what he could do with the money – all for an hour a day and no bother about finding a place to suss and finding the market for the loot and having the scuffers on to you. *Had* to get the wingy to speak

47

for him. *Had* to get Billy to get a team together. *Had* to be in Prinney Park by ten on Saturday.

He was just drifting off to sleep when Suzie started muttering and suddenly started up and began screaming again.

"Shurrup, tatty-'ead!" he said and went over to her. "Shurrup! Yer'll have me mam in!"

Suzie sobbed, calmed down and went to sleep. She's not over it yet, he thought, and wondered what kind of person he was looking for who could attack a child like Suzie in a vicious way. She would probably *never* get over it.

Eventually he went to sleep and dreamed about a woman who kept on popping up and shouting "Good!" and a large Beastly Wobbly who came after him making a noise like a motor-bike and turned out to be Joey. He woke up sweating. Must have been that pizza, he thought. Must have been off. Complain to Pa Richardson and maybe get his money back.

CHAPTER

5

Because of the nightmares, Rocky got up early next morning and he went cautiously out of Number 3. Murky Evans was at the top of the Steps.

"Be hearin' from yer," he said, as Rocky passed.

"Yer'll wait a long time," retorted Rocky, though he wasn't feeling all that certain. Then he shook it off. Joey wasn't coming home. Nothing to worry about. Murky's got the wrong message.

In Larkspur Lane, Pa Richardson was just opening, so he went in.

"Hi, dem pizzas I bought from yer . . ."

Pa Richardson sniffed. "What about them?"

"Was up all night, sick as a parrot."

"Well, yer (sniff) look all right. More likely what yer'd been watchin' on the box. Whole family in the (sniff) same state?"

"That's right – all of us."

"Had the doctor in?"

"No. An' since we've got over it we'll not report it, if yer give us the money back, see?"

Pa Richardson stepped back and looked thoughtfully round his shop, considering the matter. "I know," he concluded, "yer think yer can (sniff) con anybody, but yer see, I'm the (sniff) exception because of a lot of experience. Those pizzas, as far as I'm concerned, were in good condition when sold. Now there could have been the storing of them by yer mam. Or they could have been sold ter me by the manufacturers in faulty condition. But, only thing to do is get the doctor in an' he (sniff) will report the matter to the health authorities, if necessary. Now if yer've only come in here ter complain, I'm busy. Hello, Mrs Fletcher. What can I get you?" he greeted an early customer.

"Havin' trouble wid *him*?"

"Always trouble. Think they know it all these days (sniff) an' they don't."

"Rip off!" Rocky shouted. "They cost a lot!"

"Well, I've give yer good advice. You act on it. Now, Mrs Fletcher . . ."

Rocky went out and slammed the door, angry because Pa Richardson had got the better of him and he hadn't got his money back. He's gettin' too old for the job, he concluded.

The Cats were assembled outside the newsagent's shop. Rocky felt happier – he'd got a free day and a possible job. "Hi!" he shouted.

"Hi!" shouted Billy, Beady and Little Chan.

"How's she? Suzie?" asked Billy.

"Not good. Still looks as if she shot into a brick wall at sixty miles an hour. Scuffers haven't found out who done it, but," he added seriously. Then he said, "Youse is standin' outside the premises of my employers."

The Nabber, who until then had been ignoring the proceedings and chewing something, suddenly took an interest. "Your *employers*? Yer must be hallucinating!"

Rocky almost told the Nabber to go into the shop and find out, then he thought he'd better be certain about the job first. Anyway, the Nabber wouldn't make a good impression.

"I'm gettin' a paper round," he said impressively.

The Cats were impressed, but puzzled. It didn't seem the right thing for Rocky.

The Nabber was less impressed. "An' when do we see you trottin' round with yer big orange bag? And how much they payin' yer?"

"Those things is bein' negotiated. An' it's *my* business."

"So yer haven't got it?"

"The job is mine," retorted Rocky and added, "Goin' ter sag school and go downtown. Youse lot comin'?"

"Yer was doin' dat yesterday, but," said the Nabber. "An' it was another of yer famous failures."

Rocky ignored him. "I'm saggin'," he repeated. "Anybody comin'?"

But Little Chan couldn't because his father would expect an account of what he had done at school that day and Beady Martin said his mother would batter him if she found out and Billy didn't like going downtown because of his tricycle. He didn't say so, but Rocky understood.

"All right den," he said, "but the wingy wants a trainin' session in Prinney Park Saturday mornin'. Can yer get a team tergether, Billy?"

Billy considered the matter. He was manager of the Cats team.

"Not easy just now, Rocky," he said, "but der's some from the Buildings kick a ball about in the courtyard. Could try them. Don't seem bad."

"Dat's great, Billy. An' der wingy'll know if

51

dey're goin' ter be any good. Right. I'll gerroff downtown. Youse all have a good day!"

Deliberately he didn't invite the Nabber to accompany him, but walked along Larkspur Lane. Then he heard the Nabber.

"Yer goin' by yerself? Not with tatty-'ead?"

Rocky waved his confirmation.

"Yer carryin'?"

"Got a bit. But I'm not payin' fer passengers."

"Right. Yer on. See youse some time," the Nabber added to Billy, Beady and Little Chan, who all agreed to this and went on to school.

The bus shelter on Princes Boulevard was currently windowless and seatless but with a wealth of information and explanatory illustrations in the graffiti on its walls, inside and out, and a good selection of papers, cans and take-away trays on the floor.

"S'Buckingham Palace," Rocky commented, reading the messages. "Wonder who Lisa was and how long she waited for Alex." Then the thought of the free day ahead started him off and he shouted, "Hi, Nabber! Beat yer to the top!"

"Top of what?"

"What top's around?" Rocky started scrambling up the side of the bus shelter and sat on top. He was eventually joined by the Nabber. "Took yer time," he commented.

"Yer cheated. Gave yerself a start."

"Well, yer have ter be ready for anythin'."

"You're one ter talk." The Nabber contemplated things. "Nice view from here," he said in a polite voice.

"Borin'," said Rocky.

"S'not," said the Nabber. "Look at all der traffic an' der people."

"Lookin'," said Rocky. "An' where's der bus?"

"What about that place yer sussin'?" asked the Nabber. "When'll we do it?"

"Sussin' it."

"Takin' yer time. What about the paper round, but?"

"Der wingy'll get it for me. Said he would. Yer have ter have somebody ter speak for yer, see? Dey don't just take anybody on."

"Yer goin' ter get inter the system, you are. End up wearin' a tie."

"Listen, holler head, Flanagan's not in der system an' me mam's not for that matter. Your dad *is*, but," Rocky added. "That loo yer've got in the bathroom downstairs – yer dad was inter that system, wasn't he? A lot, comin' back from curry an' der boozer."

"My dad's on top of his job and makin' money."

"In der system. Hi," Rocky went on, "gorra piece of paper? Yer have ter have a notebook on yer, goin' ter school."

Reluctantly, the Nabber produced a notebook and offered Rocky a sheet out of it. "What yer on about now?"

Rocky rolled the paper into a ball. "I'm dropping this on the head of the next person comes past an' *you* have ter do the same ter the next person after that – you have ter hit the next one, see? Bet yer a pound I get a hit an' you don't."

"Yer gorra pound?"

"*You* got one? Feller comin' along," and Rocky, lying flat on the roof of the shelter, dropped the

53

paper ball neatly on the head of a man below, who looked startled, but didn't see them.

"Gorrim!" said Rocky.

The Nabber was ready for the next one, a woman whom the Nabber missed.

"That's a round pound yer owe me," said Rocky.

"Haven't got one. Wasn't fair, anyway. Yours was walkin' slower."

"Settle for a fifty."

"Haven't gorra . . ."

Rocky wasn't listening. The school's crossing lady was just packing up for the morning, and *she* might have seen something. Have to ask her . . .

"What yer mutterin' about?" demanded the Nabber. "Suzie, in't it? Goin' mad, in't yer?"

But the bus had drawn up and the door slid open. The driver, who happened to be Beady Martin's uncle, leaned out towards them from the driver's seat.

"You two comin' into dis vehicle or findin' alternative transport?" he asked.

"We're comin'," Rocky said, and he and the Nabber dropped down from the top of the shelter, and started to get into the bus. Then Rocky stopped because there was a shout of "Rocky!" and Suzie was racing towards them.

"Not again!" the Nabber groaned.

"Yer can't come, Suzie. Go back home," urged Rocky. "Yer not well."

"Come wid yer, Rocky," Suzie pleaded.

"Who did that to her face?" asked Beady's uncle, shocked.

"Don't know. She was mugged," said Rocky.

Beady's uncle muttered something unrepeatable and then gave them an ultimatum. "I'm sorry about that, but I've got a schedule to keep to if I want ter keep der job. I know you two gentlemen don't need to concern yerselves with such things, being free an' independent spirits, no doubt with independent incomes. You have one second before I get this bus goin' again."

"Come on, Suzie," said Rocky, giving in.

The Nabber groaned again, but followed them on to the bus.

"Yer know what'll happen?" he said. "The scuffers downtown'll take one look at her face an' take us in for questionin' on the grounds of child molestation."

"Yer've been havin' some education – was it from dat school dey threw yer out of?" demanded Rocky sarcastically.

"We could get her an eye patch," suggested the Nabber.

"Nothin' ter do wid you," retorted Rocky. "Thing is ter find out who done it to her. She said somethin' about a woman in a box, didn't yer, tatty-'ead?"

Suzie was absorbed in enjoying the bus journey and didn't reply.

"What yer on about?" demanded the Nabber. "Woman in a box? Yer believe that, yer'll believe anythin'!"

"Suzie's not daft," retorted Rocky.

"Could of fooled me."

They got off at Renshaw Street and started into the city centre.

"Tell yer what," said Rocky, "we could do some collectin' for Suzie. Brill idea."

"What yer mean?"

"All dese people. She's a deservin' cause, an' all she's had for her injuries is forty pence from the wingy and chocolates from Pa Richardson. Hi, Suzie, yer want ter make some money?"

Suzie looked up at him with her bruised face and nodded furiously.

"Yer mightn't like it, but."

"Like it," Suzie decided. "All mine!"

"Yer can't beat her for tryin'," said Rocky. "Have ter have a collectin' box."

"What yer mean?"

"Well, yer can't collect for a good cause without a collectin' box. An' der's that shoe shop over there."

The Nabber was inclined to get interested in the display of shoes in the entrance to the shop and so was Suzie, who put one shoe in her pocket, but Rocky went straight in and put on his appealing look.

"Missus," he said to the assistant, "have yer gorra spare shoe box?"

"Well, I'm not sure . . ."

"Just fer me mam, see. She's sendin' a present to her sister an' she hasn't got nothin' ter put it in and we haven't got money for buying a new one."

"Well." The assistant considered. "I'll have a look," and she returned with a box.

"Great!" Rocky was enthusiastic. "Thanks very much. Me mam'll be that happy." And he departed, collecting Nabber and removing from Suzie's pocket the shoe she had picked up.

"Know yer've got a funny face," he said, "but yer've got two feet – matchin'."

Rocky got out his pocket-knife and carefully

56

cut a money-sized slit in the top of the box and
they took up a position at the main entrance of
Lewis's and looked angry, while Suzie, without
trying, looked ferocious.

"Dat's no good, Suzie! Yer've got to look
pathetic. Like this," and Rocky drooped his
shoulders and looked down at the pavement.
Suzie imitated him.

"That's not bad, tatty-'ead, but keep yer face up
a bit. Dey have ter see yer black eye and the
bruises. That's it. Right, Nabber?"

"Give it a try." But the Nabber sounded unen-
thusiastic.

"Oh, come on!" And Rocky approached a passing shopper, pleadingly. "Give us a contribution
for me sister, missus? She's been mugged an' she
needs help," and Rocky held out the shoe box,
without much success.

"Here," said the Nabber, getting involved,
"here's forty pence – clink dem in der box –
encourage people. But I'll want them back."

Rocky tried again, clinking the box. "Give us
a contribution for me sister, missus? She's been
mugged – yer can see."

The woman shopper stopped and looked at the
three of them. "If she needs help, der's the police
and the DSS. And why are you two not at school?
And," she added, looking more closely at Rocky,
"you're an O'Rourke, aren't you? Couldn't mistake that hair. From round Larkspur Lane?"

Rocky thought fast. "No, missus. I'm a Flanagan – from Knotty Ash."

"Wherever you come from, yer should get her
home."

"Givin' this up," muttered the Nabber. "Doin'

somethin' like dis wid you's like doin' it with Prince Charles on a walkabout."

"Come on, Nabber. Yer not tryin'."

"All right," said the Nabber, and said fiercely to a harmless passing pensioner, "Hi, mister, give a contribution for this young girl what's been beaten up an' needs help!"

Fearfully, the pensioner fumbled in his pocket and dropped twenty pence in the box.

"Thanks very much," said the Nabber sarcastically.

"Yer bossin' too much," said Rocky. "Not get anywhere wid it. Got ter *plead*."

They both pleaded, and quite a lot of coins clinked into the box. Then a lush rumbled unsteadily over to them.

"Haven't got yer tambourines," he remarked, "but yer could give me a handout – haven't a place ter stay in and no money for a cup of tea."

"Clear off, mister," said Rocky. "We're collectin', not givin'."

"But the Sally Army . . ."

At that moment Rocky noticed two policemen coming towards them.

"Gerrout, Nabber," he muttered. "Come on, tatty-'ead," and they lost themselves in the crowds and made for the safety of Gina's Ice-Cream Parlour. Outside, they investigated the contents of the box – it was almost four pounds.

"Not bad," said Rocky. "Could do it again."

"Not worth it. Exhaustin'," said the Nabber.

"Mine." Suzie, who was in fact nobody's fool, held out her hand.

"Listen, tatty-'ead, was me invented dis, an' me

an' the Nabber worked on it as well as you did, so we split three ways. All right?"

Suzie looked doubtful, but then nodded agreement and they went into Gina's, where the ice-creams on offer were tremendous. When they left, Suzie sicked up all her ice-cream on the pavement. The Nabber was disgusted and looked away, but Rocky put his arm round Suzie.

"All right, tatty-'ead?" he asked. "Yer all right? Shouldn't have brung yer downtown."

"All right," said Suzie, though she didn't look it. "Go home."

"Goin' home."

They went upstairs on the bus and were very subdued, but Suzie wasn't sick again, only pale and asleep. Rocky was gazing out of the window, not looking at anything, just thinking about Suzie and Joey and what he could do. Then, when they were going along Princes Boulevard, he suddenly sat up. The bus had stopped and he saw two men walking on the other side of the Boulevard. Rocky gave the Nabber a push.

"Hi, look at that!" he said.

"Look at what?"

"Well, too late now, but I think I saw our Joey an' one of his mates back there!" And he craned his neck, trying to see.

The Nabber yawned. "Yer've got your Joey on the brain. In Spain, in't he? An' better stay there or we'll have the Crown Street Gang on to us. Be chaos."

Rocky sat back. "Looked like him, but. Looked brown."

"Delusion time," said the Nabber, but Rocky

wasn't certain about that. Too many rumours about Joey going round. Maybe he *was* back.

They got Suzie to St Catherine's Square and the Nabber departed, relieved to be out of it all.

Mrs Flanagan wasn't at home. Rocky sat Suzie down on the stairs and went up to see Ellen.

"What's it, Rocky?" she asked. "Yer mam out again?"

"Yes, an' Suzie's not well – been sick."

"Where?"

"Upper Parley."

Ellen looked angry. Then she said, "Look, Rocky, whatever yer mam say's yer'll both come inter my place an' have a cup of tea an' Suzie'll have a rest. What yer want ter take her downtown for, but? Yer know she wasn't well. Bad as yer mam, you are."

"Not dat, Ellen," Rocky protested. "Was Suzie. She wanted ter come . . ."

"What's the police doin' about Suzie?"

"Nothin' much."

"Sit down," said Ellen, "and, Suzie, you come inter the bedroom."

The last word Rocky heard from Ellen was "Disgustin'."

As he drank the tea Ellen had provided, Rocky decided he had to persuade his mother to take Suzie to see a doctor. He would have to try to find out who beat her up himself. Suddenly, he thought of Betty Mulloney – she knew everything that went on! He'd go to the Baptist Youth Club that night to see her!

"Yer mam's back. Seen her from the window. Yer'd better get off. An' don't tell her yer've been up here," said Ellen, bringing Suzie and Trevor out of the bedroom.

"Thanks, Ellen. Yer a good skin. Come on, tatty-'ead," and Rocky went to face his mother. She was unpacking some groceries and said angrily, "Wur've *you* been?"

"Locked out. An' Suzie's not well. Yer should get der doctor to her. If she's like this when Flanagan comes back der'll be trouble."

Mrs Flanagan looked at Suzie and thought about it. Then she concluded, "Yer right. I'll get her ter the doctor."

Next day, they went to the doctor, who turned out to be a young man with long hair tied behind with a ribbon, which fascinated Suzie. She couldn't take her eyes off him, but she didn't say anything, which didn't matter because Mrs Flanagan didn't stop talking until the doctor gave it up and gave Suzie some sedatives.

"Nice feller that," Mrs Flanagan concluded. "He's new der. I'll go back to him."

Well, Rocky thought, the sedatives could come in useful for his mother when Joey came home and Murky Evans got him.

But it couldn't have been Joey he saw, he decided. Joey would be straight home wanting freebies.

The Youth Club hadn't changed much, he concluded. The aerobic fanciers were wearing themselves out enthusiastically, the billiards were going and the darts, and there was a small group in a corner having what looked like a serious discussion about something serious. One thing had changed, though. Betty Mulloney was no longer serving tea – she was supervising somebody else who was serving tea.

"'Lo der, Betty," he said, being friendly. "How's it?"

"Don't let him have any tea," said Betty to her assistant. "He hasn't paid his subs."

"Goin' to, but. What I come in for."

"Well, yer can go straight out again. I've told Mr Rogers yer only come in this time of year ter join so yer can come ter the Christmas party. An' anyway, I'm the Chair now, and I can make decisions about what happens."

Rocky was astounded – or at least looked it. "Yer a chair, Betty? Never knew yer had four legs. Never noticed dem."

"Now listen, Rocky O'Rourke . . ."

"Didn't mean it, Betty. Come in ter ask yer somethin'. Yer know somebody mugged Suzie?"

"*Heard* about it," said Betty, primly.

"Well, I just wondered whether yer saw anythin' goin' home from school that night?"

"No."

"Yer didn't see Suzie goin' home from school?"

"No."

Real giver was Betty, Rocky thought.

"Well, d'yer know if there's gangs in the school – big girls, yer know – might have knocked her about?"

Betty drew herself up indignantly. "Not in *our* school! We don't all come from St Catherine's Square!"

"Trouble, Betty?"

It was, Rocky assumed, Mr Rogers, so he smiled and said hello. They went through the people running this outfit very fast, he concluded.

"Yes, Mr Rogers. It's Rocky O'Rourke. Told yer about him. Only comes for the Christmas party."

"S'not dat, Mr Rogers," said Rocky. "Just, yer know like, der's not enough money for me mam ter pay me subs for der whole year an' me little sister, Suzie – well, she doesn't get a lot out of life, an' a party . . ."

"He's lyin', Mr Rogers . . ."

"Do yer, Betty Mulloney," muttered Rocky.

"Now then," said Mr Rogers, "under the circumstances, I'm prepared to let you off the subs until Christmas, and if the Committee agree to your membership, and if you come regularly every week and take part, you'll be made welcome."

"But, Mr Rogers," Betty protested.

"A moment, Betty. I have to tell you, Rocky, that we're not having a Christmas party."

"Yer not havin' one *again*?" Rocky was disgusted. "I've never got ter one yet – yer always changin' things!"

"We are having," said Mr Rogers, "a pantomime."

Rocky brightened. "Well, dat'll be all right, but."

"Yes. A pantomime. And all club members will contribute to putting it on and profits will go to a charity. Now I'm sure you could help. If you don't want to act or help behind the scenes, you could sell programmes or show people to their seats."

Rocky was furious. "It's a con!" he retorted.

Mr Rogers was surprised. "No. It's all in a good cause, and . . ."

"Told yer," said Betty Mulloney with satisfaction. "Told yer about him. His family's the worst in the Square!"

"Now, Betty. Give him a chance."

"Don't want one," said Rocky. "Not worth it. Unpaid labour, dat's what it is. An' thanks for yer help over Suzie, Betty Mulloney, I *don't* think. Disgustin'." And he departed, leaving Mr Rogers upset and Betty Mulloney looking self-righteous. He weaved his way through the aerobics session, creating a certain amount of chaos, having first given the tea table a bump so as to spill some and put a darts player entirely off his stroke.

Outside, in the darkening and damp afternoon, he considered things and felt better. But he would get his own back on Betty Mulloney. Anyway, he decided, it was a boring institution and he'd never got anything out of it. But he *had* managed to pick up a packet of biscuits and some tea-bags for the hideout.

CHAPTER
6

"Right. This it, is it?" Mr Oliver surveyed the Cats' team assembled in Princes Park. He looked a bit dubious. "Didn't get the best on the market to make up the numbers, did yer, Billy?"

"Norra lot *on* the market, Mr Oliver. But I've seen them in action – think there's possibilities. Need some trainin'."

"Don't all of us? All right. Fitness first, skills next. Warm up, runnin' on the spot, after the whistle. Keep yerselves spread out!"

It seemed to the Cats that the wingy was never going to blow the stop whistle.

"Long way ter go," Mr Oliver commented with satisfaction. "Now yer'll not need yer jog suits or anoraks for the next, which is runnin'. Runnin' round this area of grass. I'm not lookin' for speed just now. Lookin' for stamina. Right. On the whistle."

When it blew again, the Cats came slowly and breathlessly towards Mr Oliver. "Get out of breath cleanin' yer teeth, you lot would," he commented. "Yer can listen while yer get it back. Now passin', as I've tried to get inter yer heads, is the most important aspect of the game – yer can't practise it too much. Now watch. Yer'll have ter imagine me lost arm, see? Now it's right foot ter the ball, left arm across the body, right arm behind for balance. Head down. Eyes on the ball. Know who yer passin' to. Got it? Right. Yer'll be in threes – one passin', one receivin' an' an interceptor. Spread out an' . . ."

"Hi! It's the kittens!" a voice shouted. It was Chick, leader of Chick's Lot, and his loyal supporter, Spadge. "Yer mams let yer out 'cos yer've been good little kittens?"

Mr Oliver shouted to them, "Clear off! . . . Now!"

"They want the champagne life on a lemonade income," Spadge contributed, "so dey can't afford a whole coach, see?" And they both fell about laughing.

"Ignore them," said Mr Oliver. "They'll get tired."

"No," said Rocky, "dey won't. Only one thing," and he strode over to Chick and Spadge and stared fiercely at them, his red hair flaming.

"Listen, I'll chin youse," he said to them quietly. "Nobody says dat kind of thing about Mr Oliver. *He* was a star player for the 'Pool. We're goin' ter take youse out. So clear off. An' yer'll be hearin' from me, wacks!"

Chick's eyes narrowed. "Yer on," he said. "An' we'll see who does the takin' out. Come on, Spadge. We're interruptin' the kittens' exercise."

"Showed youse before who was kittens!" Rocky shouted after them. "Show youse again!"

The only response was some expressive gestures from Chick and Spadge.

Rocky went back to the Cats. "Sorry 'bout dat, Mr Oliver."

"Well," said Mr Oliver, "yer very impressive.

I'm impressed! Now youse can all impress me with some passin'."

"Mr Oliver . . ." Rocky said as they went back to St Catherine's Square.

"How's Suzie? Said anythin'?"

"Nothin' that makes sense. But, Mr Oliver . . ."

"Think yer team'll shape up. Better think about arrangin' some matches. Any other teams about?"

"Well, there's the Bone-Breakers, but I don't know much about dem, an' der's the Allsorts. But, Mr Oliver . . ."

"An' there's Chick's Lot. We could put *them* down."

"But, Mr Oliver," Rocky said desperately, and the wingy grinned and put his hand on Rocky's shoulder.

"Stop worryin'. I'm goin' for a pint an' I'll have a word about you when I pick me paper up. Right?"

Rocky was relieved and then jubilant. "Great! S'great! Thanks, Mr Oliver. Yer a good skin!"

"But don't forget your terms of employment. See yer, Rocky."

"An' don't *you* forget ter stop at one pint," retorted Rocky, knowing the wingy's weakness.

"Thanks for remindin' me!"

Rocky turned to the Cats Gang who were following. "Gorrit!" he shouted. "The job! Gorrit!"

"Them newsagents must be innercents or missionaries," the Nabber commented.

"Congrats, Rocky," said Billy. "Come round wid yer one mornin'."

"Thanks, wack. But I'm not certain till I go an' see dem." And I'm not certain, he thought, suddenly doubtful, whether I can do the job. "Hi,"

67

he said. "Let youse know. Hideout this afternoon?"

But the Cats didn't seem keen. Beady had relatives coming, Little Chan was going to the Chinese centre to practise his flute, Billy and his brother were being taken out to get some clothes and the Nabber was not interested unless Rocky had the funds to throw a party to celebrate. Rocky hadn't.

"Yer a rotten lot," he concluded.

He got to Number 3 just as his mother arrived from the launderette with a large plastic bag of clothes and Suzie, who was looking tired.

"All right, tatty-'ead?" he asked. Suzie smiled.

"Notice yer don't ask about me," grumbled his mother, "and *I've* been washing all yer clothes. Come on, get yourselves in."

As they went into their flat, Rocky picked up a postcard that the postman had pushed under the door. It had a picture of a steep, narrow street of white houses with balconies with flowers on them, but the stamp was British. On the card was written: "Back soon. Need bed. Joey."

Without a word Rocky gave it to his mother.

"That's smashin'," she exclaimed happily. "He's comin' . . ." Then her voice trailed off and she looked at Rocky.

"That's right. S'not smashin'," said Rocky. "It's the end. Better move out to somewhere a long way away – like New Brighton."

"We should warn Joey," said Mrs Flanagan, "'bout dat feller – what's his name?"

"Murky Evans," said Rocky resignedly. "How we do it, but? We don't know where Joey is."

"Well – in Spain."

68

"Big country. An' dey don't sell British stamps. What's der ter eat?"

Mrs Flanagan dropped the bag of washing and sat down in despair. "Don't know where to turn," she said. "Don't want Joey harmed." And she began to cry.

Rocky and Suzie watched her, not knowing what to do. Then Rocky said, "Listen, mam. We'll have some tea an' some butties an' den we can have a talk about Joey. See, I can't ask der Scuffers to look after our Joey, because dat's what dey want ter do – in Walton Jail. An' I can't get Mr Oliver involved. The only thing is, when Joey appears, we warn him an' get him off."

Mrs Flanagan dried her eyes. "Yer right, Rocky, an' I'll make some tea. But if I ever meet up wid dat Murky Evans, I'll batter him round the Square."

"Wouldn't try it, mam. He's a big feller."

Must have been Joey he saw from the bus, Rocky thought. Must be home, and Murky would be after him even more for information.

That afternoon he went down to the newsagents to suss things out. The fat woman and the man with the granny bicycles on his nose both smiled at him.

"'Bout der paper round," he said hopefully.

"Yes. What we thought, Rocky, was that tomorrow you could do the round with John – he's the lad's been doin' it and his last day was today, but he'll come and take you tomorrow. Be here at seven – all right? An' then you'll know whether you want to take it on and we'll give you a week at it to make sure. All right?"

"Well," said Rocky, "thought I'd got it, what wid all dem conditions. But all right. I'll agree to *dem* conditions on one condition."

"What's that?" asked the man with the granny bicycles.

"Get a free comic every week."

They looked at him, then at each other.

"Get the first week over, then we'll see," said the woman.

Rocky was disappointed. He'd expected something definite. It's like trying to get a job as security guard to the Prime Minister, he grumbled to himself, but when he passed Pa Richardson's he saw that there were some men still working in the shop next door, so he went in. They weren't actually working – they were drinking tea and eating sandwiches.

"'Lo der," he said innocently. "Got the place finished?"

"Clear off, son," said one of them.

"Haven't come ter pinch yer butties," he said, indignantly. "Just want ter ask about de place. Me grandad used ter own it, see?"

This was untrue, but Rocky thought it might create some sympathy and interest, which it appeared to do.

"Yer grandad? When was that?"

"Well, I was only 'bout dis high, but I used ter come round de place. He sold fruit an' veg, me grandad. Just wondered what was happenin' to it."

The man considered for a moment and then said, "Shouldn't be tellin' yer, but it's goin' ter be a jewellery shop – lot different from fruit an' veg." And he winked at the other men, who grinned, though Rocky did not notice this – he was too astounded.

"Jewellers? In Larkspur Lane?" Rocky's amazement was genuine. "In Larkspur Lane? Be another take-away!"

"Yer don't know the security that's goin' in here, so don't get any ideas."

"Didn't have none. Hi, yer mind if I have a look round? Won't get another chance."

"Help yerself."

And Rocky did. He went over the place – the two rooms downstairs, the room upstairs. There was a window at the back upstairs, which might be useful as an entry, and a back door downstairs, which might also be useful. On the other hand there was the security. As he was leaving, watched with some amusement by the workmen, he was wondering whether Nabber Neville had any contacts in the secondhand jewellery trade. He contemplated what he could do with the money from the paper round. Compared with jewellery, the paper round was nothing!

"Seen what yer want?" the man in charge asked. "Because we've finished here now."

"Yes, thanks."

"Only I have ter tell yer I have ter report yer looked round der place – security, yer know like."

That bothered Rocky. "Do what yer like."

"Well, I'll need yer name."

"Name's me own business," and Rocky ran off, a bit worried, and hearing the men laughing behind him. The Nabber didn't have any idea, he thought, what sussing a place involved.

Sunday morning at seven, Larkspur lane was lamp-

71

lit and deserted – more deserted than he'd ever seen it before. But the lights in the newsagent's were a beacon and inside was the man behind the counter and a couple of boys collecting large orange sacks of newspapers. Was interesting, Rocky thought. Was different. So he greeted them with a "'lo der. How's it?" and the man behind the counter said, "Ah, Rocky. Now this is John. He'll take you round his area."

John wasn't impressive. Rocky wasn't tall – he was the shortest of the Cats Gang except for Little Chan, but John was shorter. And he was thin, his face narrow and pointed, but he had a determined look.

"Come on, den," he said. "Yer'd better carry the bag ter get used to it. Always heavy on a Sunday."

"Right, wack. Let's have it. Yer been doin' dis long?" asked Rocky.

"Two years." John wasn't a very communicative person, Rocky concluded. "Der's quite a few drops in St Catherine's Buildings," John went on. "The stairs is a nuisance."

They went up the stairs in the silent building, pushing newspapers through inadequate letter-boxes. They put a newspaper into the flat Billy lived in.

"Joseph Terrace next," said John. "Don't like it."

"Got some good enemies round there," said Rocky. "Know Chick's Lot?"

"Never here long enough ter know anybody. Not many drops."

Joseph Terrace was, if anything, more sinister at that time in the morning than it was late at night when the pub was turning out. Nobody was around, it was silent and you couldn't read the graffiti on the walls of the empty houses opposite the flats.

"Prinney Boulevard next," said John. "This is the dangerous part."

But the Boulevard looked safe to Rocky, who had seen it at its worst when you could hardly get across because of the traffic. Now there was only the occasional car or taxi.

"What's dangerous about this?" he asked. "Here, this bag's dead heavy."

"Can affect yer shoulders," said John unemotionally. "Dangerous because I was mugged here once. Three fellers. Thought I had money, but I hadn't because I don't collect, see? Dey pay at the shop. But dey didn't believe me. Got knocked about."

"Was it the Crown Street Gang?" asked Rocky.

"No, it wasn't dem. I live next door to Murky Evans."

Rocky was astounded. "How'd yer do dat an' still live?" he asked.

"S'all right, is Murky, when he's not in a mood."

This was new light on Murky, and Rocky began to view John with more respect.

"Other thing put me off," John continued in a monotone. "Kerb crawlers. Dazzle yer with der headlights an' dey try ter get yer inter the cars. Had to fight one off an' dat's when me mam an' me decided I had ter give the round up. Gorra job at a supermarket. Fillin' shelves. Borin' but safer. Now dis house dey've gorra big dog. If he's out in front I don't deliver, just throw the paper inter the garden an' he shreds it. Watch out for him. Dis house is a funny one – just started few days ago with papers. Three every day. Never seen nobody around."

The next house had its windows boarded up and the garden looked like a fill-in site for cans, bottles, papers, cardboard boxes and a supermarket trolley.

"Don't take papers, der," said John.

"Gorrenough of dem already," said Rocky.

There were only a few deliveries after that and John said there were no problems. At the turn-off to St Catherine's Square, he said, "Yer can get back yerself? Hope yer get the round. In der summer it's fine. An' if yer want any advice I'm in der Spar shop in Allerton, evenin's and Saturday mornin's."

"Right, wack. An' thanks. See yer. Terra, well."

Could be a good contact, John, Rocky thought as he went towards Larkspur Lane. Might have information about the Spar shop which could be useful if he decided to do it, and was a contact with Murky Evans, if needed. He went cheerfully into the newsagent's and dropped his sack beside the counter.

"All right den? I gorrit done. So der job's mine?" he asked.

"We did say," said the man with the granny bicycles, "a week's trial."

"Listen, mister," retorted Rocky, "from what I see of it dis is casual, sweated labour an' very dangerous. I should be askin' for insurance, so yer can ferget the week's trial or I'm not interested. An' the agreement *will* include a free *Eagle* every week."

The man smiled. "Right. You have the job and the comic. But any slip up and you're off."

"Won't be none. An' if I'm not paid I *will* be off! An' if yer don't mind I'll have me *Eagle* now!"

It was daylight when he sprinted up the Steps, thinking that he would have a sleep, then tell the Cats about the jeweller's shop on the Lane, and find out exactly where Suzie was beaten up. He was feeling jubilant, but at the top of the Steps there was a small gathering: Murky Evans and two of his gang.

"Hi, Murky!" Rocky shouted.

Murky didn't say anything – he only watched him.

"Me name's Rocky, not Joey!" Rocky shouted, but he got no response and he was sweating as he strolled past them.

In Number 3, Mrs Flanagan was sitting in front of the electric fire having her first cup of tea of the day. She looked at Rocky in astonishment.

"Wur've yer been this time of the mornin'?" she asked. "Yur've not been out all night? Because if yer start that . . ."

"Course I haven't. What'd I be out all night for? Gorrup early, dat's all, so I went for a walk. How's Suzie?"

"See for yourself."

Suzie was still asleep.

Rocky helped himself to some tea, which he needed, and also some toast, and wondered what he should tell his mother. It could get to her that he was doing the paper round. But the most important thing was Joey and Murky Evans.

"Yer know, Rocky," said his mother, contemplating her tea, "I don't know where ter turn next. Der's that business wid Suzie, der's dat note through der door an' der's Joey comin' back. But der's nothin' from Flanagan."

Rocky contemplated *his* tea. "Be all right, mam," he said. "Always is. Suzie'll be all right an' Flanagan'll come back. Always does. An' Joey'll come. Only, mam, I wouldn't put it around dat yer expect him."

"Why not, but? He's done very well an' I want Ellen-from-upstairs and *her* from Number 4 ter know dat!"

"Look, mam," Rocky went to the window. "See dem der?"

"Who's dem? Just some layabouts."

"Dey're after Joey. Dat's Murky an' his gang."

"After Joey? What for, but? After his money?"

"I told yer, mam – after *him*."

Mrs Flanagan fell back in her chair. "Oh, my God," she said. "What would anybody want ter be after Joey for? He's a good lad."

"Well," Rocky said, "I wouldn't worry all that much. Joey's always come through all right."

Mrs Flanagan sat up. "Yer right, Rocky. He has. I'll have another cup of tea an' then I'll go down ter the police in Larkspur Lane and tell them they have ter look after Joey."

"Mam," Rocky said, "I told yer! Yer haven't got ter tell the scuffers anything about our Joey!"

CHAPTER
7

It wasn't, Rocky decided as he got out of bed, the kerb-crawlers and the alsatian that would put him off the job; it was getting up in the dark and cold. He crept into the next room, carefully lifted the alarm clock from the mantelpiece and took it to the window to try to see the time by the light from the lamp outside, hoping the clock wouldn't go off and wake his mother. He was going to be in time. Must get a clock, he thought. Then he quietly opened the cupboard door and felt around for Joey's torch – he might need it, if only as a weapon, but he was pretty certain Murky Evans wouldn't be doing night-shift. Nevertheless, he ran all the way down the Steps to Larkspur Lane. It was empty except for a man walking a little dog and a milk float purring smoothly along. But the newsagent's was a brightly-lit hive of activity.

Inside the shop there was a youth of about sixteen in charge, sorting newspapers and handing out orange bags to a group of boys. He looked suspiciously at Rocky. "Who are you?"

"Rocky O'Rourke. Who are you?" demanded Rocky.

"Boss of this show in the morning. Yer name's on the list – 'new to the job but knows the round'," he read out. "Right?"

"Dat's clever," said Rocky. "Yer can read as well!"

"Now listen, kid . . ."

"Norra kid. Rocky O'Rourke – run der Cats Gang. An' what's *your* monniker?"

The boss contemplated him. "Right. Heard about you. Yer'll of heard about me – Blair Turner – run the Bone-Breakers."

"Great," said Rocky. "Yer gorra footy team goin'?"

"Pound your lot inter der ground."

"Be in touch. Give's me bag."

"Listen, Rocky," said Blair, as he handed it over, "I come down Joseph Terrace this mornin'. There's trouble there."

"Thanks for der warnin'. See yer."

Always trouble in Joseph's, Rocky thought as he pulled the heavy bag on to his shoulder. Maybe Chick and Spadge were having an early morning session. He walked along Larkspur Lane towards Joseph Terrace wondering whether he could claim danger money from his employers.

St Catherine's Buildings had some lights on, but it was quiet. As he reached the door of the flat where Billy lived, it opened.

"Hi, Rocky!" said Billy, still in his pyjamas. "How's it?"

"Slave labour," said Rocky, though he was really enjoying the strangeness and feeling of danger. "Listen, skin, a feller called Blair Turner's runnin' the Bone-Breakers an' he seems all right and's got a team."

"Wur's he from, but?"

"Find out. Trouble in Joseph's."

78

"Was a lot of noise a bit back. Want me ter come round wid yer?"

"Norrin yer 'jamas! See yer."

Joseph Terrace *was* in turmoil – more like turning-out time than seven fifteen in the morning.

The pub and the off-licence had their lights on and so had a lot of flats in the Terrace. There were people out on balconies and some on the pavement in an assortment of overcoats and dressing-gowns, and there were babies crying in every direction. There were three police cars and an ambulance, all with flashing lights.

"Where yer goin', son?"

Rocky looked up at the policeman. "Deliver der papers."

"Not today you're not. You get on to your next drop."

Rocky was interested. "What's goin' on, but?" he asked. "Hi! Der's der fire brigade!"

That distracted the policeman, so Rocky hung about. Interest seemed to be centred on a point halfway up the flats where a man was standing on the balcony and shouting. Then he shot back inside and after a bit re-appeared and flung something down. It was an electric cooker and it smashed resoundingly on the pavement. In a few minutes he was back and deposited a television set. There was a bit of a pause then, until he re-appeared and tipped a wardrobe down.

"Think he's movin' house, but?" Rocky asked the policeman.

"Told yer ter move *on*!"

Rocky cupped his hands round his mouth and

shouted up to the man, who was now balancing a small fridge on the balcony railing, "Hi, mister! Yer waitin' fer yer paper delivery?"

The man paused. "Never had one."

"Got one for yer. Hang on a bit. Here," he said to the policeman, "I can't deliver, so yer can put dis one through his letter-box. Might take his mind off things."

By comparison with Joseph's, Princes Boulevard was as peaceful as the cemetery behind the Cathedral, though the dog was out. Rocky threw him the newspaper, which he shredded. At the house next to the fill-in site, which had just started taking papers, Rocky pushed three papers through the door and was departing when someone pulled in the last of the newspapers and whispered through the letter-box, "Help me. Please help." It was a young girl's voice and she sounded desperate.

Rocky turned back to the door and pushed open the flap again. "Yer there?" he asked. "Somethin' der matter?"

But there was no reply.

At the gate he stopped to look back. Was his day for funny happenings, he decided, and went on past the boarded-up house with the boxes and the supermarket trolley on the lawn. An old woman came out of the garden, very small and thin, wearing slippers and a long coat that she kept gathering up with one hand. She didn't look at him. She just walked.

Rocky delivered another paper and made a "Gerroff, you" gesture at the flashing lights of a passing car. Lot going on, he thought. Was all right. Made you sweat. But that voice asking for help worried him.

He hoped his mother would still be in bed when he got home, but she was up, sitting by the fire drinking tea.

"Yer've not been walking out there again at this time?" she said angrily.

"Well, yer see, mam . . ." He got himself some tea and bread and butter. "It's der footy season comin' on an' we're all in trainin'."

"Well, yer could train after school."

"Well, it's gettin' dark den as well."

"Not as dark as it is now. Yer'll get yerself run over an' they'll start sayin' it's all my fault, so yer can stop it."

"Right den," said Rocky meekly, with no intention of stopping it.

In Larkspur Lane Rocky leant back on Pa Richardson's wire frames, wondering whether he'd missed the Cats – and yawning. Then he went to have a look at the shop next door that had been done up. There was a light inside and a car parked outside. He tried to peer in through the slats of the blinds, but could see nothing. The parked car had its hatchback open and there were some parcels on display inside. Rocky did not go immediately to investigate, which was just as well because a man came out of the shop then. He gave Rocky a suspicious look but went on unloading parcels into the shop.

Then he said, "What yer hangin' round here for?"

"Just waitin' for me mates, yer know, like."

The man locked the shop door, slammed down the hatchback and started to get into the car.

"What yer trading in, mister?" asked Rocky.

The man looked him fiercely in the eyes. "Listen, son, if I see you round here again . . ."

"Just me grandad used ter have dis shop – sold vegetables . . ."

"That story won't get you far. Now clear off. If I see you again I'll have the police on to you." The man got into his car and drove off at speed.

Definitely interesting, Rocky thought.

"Hi, Rocky," Billy shouted, pedalling along Larkspur Lane. "How was it? In Joseph's?"

"Chaotic. But I survived. An' listen, Billy, der's somethin' wrong in one of der houses in Prinney Boulevard. Somebody worried der. Wants help."

Billy frowned down at the handlebars of his trike. "What kind of help?" he asked.

"Don't know."

"Maybe tell the police," Billy suggested.

"Dey wouldn't believe *me*, would dey? I mean, dey'd think I was havin' dem on, wouldn't dey?"

"But if . . ." Billy sounded worried, but then Beady and Little Chan appeared, and then the Nabber, who asked, "How's der little paper-rounder doin' den?"

Rocky offered to pin one on him and the Nabber said, "All right," and he'd pin one on *him* and then Beady said, "Give it up, will youse?" So they did.

"Got things ter tell youse," Rocky said, as they walked on. "See youse in der hideout ternight."

The others went into school, but Rocky stopped to have a word with the crossing lady.

"Hi, missus," he said, "yer know my stepsister,

Suzie Flanagan? Always got a bow in her hair, an' she's a bit strange?"

"Course I know Suzie – never says anything. I heard about her being beaten up – terrible."

"Did yer see her across that day after school?"

"Yes, I did. I remember it, because she suddenly stopped dead in the middle of the road, and I had a right time getting her to move."

"Did yer see which way she went?"

"Usual way – along Prinney."

"Didn't turn off down Joseph Terrace?"

"No, no. Went straight on."

"Didn't see anything funny happening along Prinney?"

"You don't have time to look around in this job!"

"Well, thanks, missus."

That settles it, he thought as he went into school. She was mugged on the Boulevard, and Betty Mulloney must have seen *something*. Wouldn't give you anything, Betty Mulloney wouldn't. Not even the skin off a rice pudding.

The Cats' hideout was in the basement of the old vicarage at the top of the Steps down to Larkspur Lane, a place which Rocky had personally discovered. It had needed some cleaning up and whatever bits and pieces of furniture and carpets they could find, but it was secret and had to be kept secret. He kept to the rules and ran past as though he was going somewhere else, then doubled back, shot down the steps into the basement and gave the special knock on the door.

Beady opened it just enough to let Rocky in.

They'd got the candles lit and the kettle was heating on the paraffin heater.

"Hi, den," said Rocky.

"An' you," said the Nabber, shuffling the cards. "Got the job sussed?"

Rocky sat down on the old sofa. "Dat shop on Larkspur. A man was der this mornin' an' parked his car an' takes stuff out of de shop an' puts it in der back of der car an' leaves the hatchback open till he's finished."

"Interestin'," said the Nabber. "Well sussed – but where d'we go from there?"

"Have ter suss it a bit more – see how many times he goes there."

"What's der loot, but?" asked the Nabber, and began dealing.

Rocky paused impressively, to pick up his cards. Then he said casually, "Jewellery."

The Cats stopped playing and looked at him.

"Yer have ter be coddin'," said the Nabber. "How'd yer know it's jewellery?"

"Was told. Workmen in der told me an' I looked der place over – like Fort Knox."

"When were yer last at Fort Knox?" asked the Nabber sarcastically.

"Listen, Nabber, yer goin' ter have ter go inter how yer'll get rid of the jewellery."

For once the Nabber was silenced. Beady made some tea and they drank it and ate the biscuits Beady had found fallen off the back of a delivery van. While he muttered that they were running out of conny milk the other Cats thought about the matter.

"It's a big job," said Billy at last. "If it's jewellery we'll have all the police after us."

"Dey'll not know who took it, but," said Rocky. "Nobody'll see us. Soon as I've got de parcel everybody disappears – never anybody round Larkspur that early, anyway."

"If the Nabber starts sellin' it, the news *will* get round," said Beady.

"Youse got no guts!" exclaimed Rocky. "It's a *big* job – bigger than anythin' our Joey done."

"Won't be," said the Nabber, gradually recovering and pushing back on his head the new straw hat his father had bought him. "Can't be. It'll be your Joey's next biggest job, won't it? We suss, we plan, an' Joey comes in an' does it. Like the Ratman's. We're not really the Cats Gang, we're der Working-for-Joey Gang. We plan dis thing an' Joey'll be back from Spain an' do it."

Rocky was really angry at the lack of enthusiasm and because there was some truth in what the Nabber said, but he was determined to do the job.

"Joey'll not know about it. An' in dat hat yer look like a retired bee-keeper. Ferget it – all of youse. Do it meself."

"What if the man has a gun?" asked Billy.

"What for, but?"

"Defend himself against you," said the Nabber.

"Now, listen, Nabber . . ."

"Maybe," said Little Chan, "we should try it," which was amazing, because Little Chan never liked getting into trouble.

"Thanks," said Rocky. "Dat go for der lot of yer?"

The Cats agreed.

"Right," said Rocky. "We'll have a game."

85

"That house, Rocky. Prinney Boulevard," said Billy. "Have ter look into that."

"Goin' to, skin. An' dat feller in charge of der papers, Blair Turner, he's runnin' the Bone-Breakers in Granby Street an' they've definitely gorra team."

Billy was worried about Granby Street, but he said, "All right. I'll get in touch."

"An' dat's my game," said Rocky. Then it struck him that the Cats were rather quiet, rather thoughtful. "Youse all right?" he asked.

"Well," said the Nabber, sitting up and stretching, "s'all go, in't it? Unless, of course, it turns out to be all stop."

"Yer can trust me," said Rocky.

"Can trust yer ter mess it up."

Rocky looked at him through narrowed eyes, his red hair flaming in the candlelight. "Yer'll eat yer words yet," he said. And not getting any response, he left.

As the door closed behind him, the Cats got together. What had made them think was Little Chan being willing to do a jeweller's shop right opposite his father's chippy.

Little Chan hesitated, then he said, reluctantly, "My father knows about that shop and he has never said anything about jewellery."

There was a pause, then the Nabber pushed his hat back and laughed. "Another of his famous failures!" And he left.

Murky Evans was still at the top of the Steps with one of his gang. Rocky came up behind him, remembering that John, who'd had the newspaper round before him, thought that Murky was all right.

"Joey back?" asked Murky.

"No. Not comin' back. But I wanted ter ask yer. Me step-sister was beaten up the other day on Prinney Boulevard. Know anyone might of done it? Suzie's only seven and not carryin' money."

Murky Evans frowned. "She the one that threw that half-brick at me at the Ratman's?"

"Well yes, but . . ."

"Got some guts den, hasn't she? I'll ask around." He looked at Rocky with his determined brown eyes. "What about Joey?"

Rocky rubbed his hands through his red hair. "Nothin' about Joey. Told yer."

"I'll keep watchin'."

Maybe John was right about Murky, Rocky thought. Had his good side.

Rocky's mother was beside the fire, watching television. Suzie was sitting at the table drawing again with Rocky's red biro. For a moment he thought she was drawing on one of his mother's paper-backed romances, but it was only on one of his comics. He dropped down on the sofa.

"All right, tatty-'ead?" he asked Suzie, and she nodded.

But his mother was in a mood. "Oh," she said. "It's the lodger back! Thought yer'd took off! Yer never in this place – out all hours, mornin' an' night! It'll have ter stop!"

"Not doin' nothin' wrong, but – just wid me mates."

"I'll have *just wid yer mates!*" Mrs Flanagan began to shout. "Wait till Flanagan comes back!"

Suzie stared at her and then shouted, "Not fight! Not fight! Bad!" And she started to cry.

Mrs Flanagan was amazed. "What's up wid her?" she asked.

"She's still not got over bein' beaten up, has she? It's been a shock. S'all right, tatty-'ead."

Suzie looked up at him, rubbing the tears away. Then she showed him what she'd been drawing. It was the house again with the woman and the long box with the round thing at one end.

"Bad, Rocky," she said, pointing to the woman, and then "Good," pointing to the box.

Rocky was mystified, but he agreed with her and she seemed satisfied.

"Make some tea, Rocky," said Mrs Flanagan. "I don't know what ter do about that gang hanging around the place an' our Joey."

"Don't do nothin'." Rocky started making tea but then there was a knock on the door.

Mrs Flanagan started up. "Who's dat? This time of night? It's dat gang . . ."

The knock was repeated and a voice said, "Constable McMahon. Can I have a word, Mrs Flanagan?"

Suzie disappeared behind the sofa and Rocky went to the door. Feeling anxious in case somehow or other McMahon had got information about his plans for that shop, Rocky was immediately on the attack.

"S'a bit late, in't it, scuffer?" he demanded.

"Calm down, Rocky. Mind if I come in, Mrs Flanagan?"

"Well – all right. What's it about, but? Is it him?" She pointed at Rocky. "Because I can't keep up wid his comin's an' goin's . . ."

"Shurrup, will yer, mam!"

"No," said McMahon, but looking interested. "It's not Rocky. It's the Crown Street Gang hanging round the Square. We've had some complaints."

"Well, I wanted ter complain, but *he* said . . ."

"Nothin' ter do wid us," said Rocky quickly.

"Nothin' ter do with your Joey?"

"Dey've got nothin' ter do wid Joey, an' anyway he's not here."

"Not comin' back?" persisted McMahon.

"No. Enjoyin' himself." But then Rocky remembered that his mother had put Joey's card on the mantelpiece and he changed his position so that the constable would not be looking straight at it.

"Hi," he said, with unusual friendliness, "have a look at this. One of Suzie's drawings. She's feelin' a lot better, yer know, like."

Constable McMahon seemed a bit suspicious but looked at the drawing.

"Yes," he said. "Very good. And that's another thing. Mrs Mulloney came to tell us that her daughter has remembered seeing some disturbance on the opposite side of Princes Boulevard when she was coming home from school – about the day Suzie was attacked."

Rocky was indignant. "Well, I asked her! I asked Betty Mulloney ter ask about it!"

"She was certain about the incident, but couldn't see who was involved because there was a car parked in the way – just heard shouts. Could be nothing to do with Suzie."

He looked again at Suzie's drawing, thoughtfully. "Might be an idea," he said to Rocky, "to walk Suzie along Princes Boulevard. She might react to the place where it happened – if it did happen there. That drawing must mean something to her. That a *coffin* she's drawn? And who's that woman waving her arms . . . ?"

"Yer can't take much notice of what Suzie draws," said Rocky. "She just imagines things."

Then he thought maybe McMahon wasn't as thick as he looked. Maybe he was on to something with Suzie's drawing. Suzie always retaliated, but in her own way – throwing half-bricks, shouting, screaming, jumping up and down and destroying his mother's books. She'd done drawings before that meant something – to her, anyway. Maybe he should take more notice of what she was trying to tell him.

CHAPTER

8

The man with the hatchback didn't take much sussing, Rocky decided. He was a man of habit and Rocky had watched him, secretly, from the doorway of Pa Richardson's shop, the Chans' doorway and the bottom of the Steps. Went like clockwork, the man did, and always put some parcels in the open boot before locking the shop up.

He got the plan worked out one morning on the paper round when it was misty and damp and the Lane and Joseph Terrace and Princes Boulevard looked particularly dangerous and mysterious. He didn't need the Cats in on his plan – they didn't deserve it or a share in the loot. But the plan would need other people to keep dowse. At least so far it *had* been a secret. He didn't want Murky Evans or Chick's Lot hearing about it, and he had a feeling that Blair wouldn't be interested.

The dog wasn't in the garden that morning, but Rocky threw the paper in just in case it suddenly appeared and so he was quite relaxed as he went next door and pushed three papers through the letter-box. Suddenly, the last one, which had stuck, was pulled in and again the voice whispered, "Help me. Please help." Sounded like a young girl.

Rocky went back up the steps to the door and pushed open the flap again. "What's der matter?"

he asked, but then the door was flung open and a fierce-looking blonde woman in a woolly dressing-gown demanded, "Who are *you*? What do you want?"

She not only sounded fierce, she sounded foreign.

"Don't want nothin', missus," Rocky retorted. "Just put yer papers through, yer know, like." And he departed. The door was slammed behind him. He didn't like the situation, but he couldn't do much about it. Maybe it was just some young girl in there making a bit of a drama to amuse herself. Anyway, she'd got somebody looking after her. Though *he* wouldn't like to be looked after by that woman. Looked as if she could batter you! It could be a dangerous situation.

At school break next morning, Rocky, feeling confident he'd got the job organized, ignored the Cats and strolled over to Blair and the Bone-Breakers. They were at the opposite end of the playing-fields from the Cats and Rocky felt sure the Cats were anxious. The Nabber looked especially anxious, chewing something and with his hat on one side.

"Hi, Blair, want to arrange a match."

"Yer on. When?"

"Gorra manager. Billy Griffiths – dat's him der. He'll get in touch. Bit nervous, but."

"Well," said Blair, "that's natural, given my position in the community. Don't worry, but. See it goes all right."

Rocky then crossed over to the Cats. "S'all right, Billy," he said. "Blair'll have a word about the match. All right?"

Billy seemed relieved. "I'll see him," he said.

"Got der job sussed. Anybody interested – hideout ternight?" and he left them.

"Yer can see," commented the Nabber, watching him go, "that his head's got bigger."

In the candlelit hideout, Rocky looked seriously at the Cats.

"That man comes every mornin' ter that shop at the same time and does the same thing – parks der car an' . . ."

"All right. We'll believe yer," yawned the Nabber, relaxed now that he knew there was no jewellery involved.

Rocky ignored him. "Plan is, if youse can manage early, day after tomorrow, I'll be around beside der car, an' if Billy's keepin' dowse outside Pa Richardson's an' Little Chan's watchin' from der chippy, an' Beady's at the bottom of the Steps, an' Nabber's halfway up, I get somethin' out of the car, pass it on ter Beady an' he passes it on ter the Nabber an' he runs wid it inter here. Anybody sees anythin' goin' wrong, give der warnin'. Hoot like an owl."

The Cats were silent, then Beady commented, "Lot of passin' an' runnin'."

"Necessary," said Rocky. "Has ter be quick."

"I have ter take into consideration," said the Nabber, "that it's me'll be in trouble if the Crown Street Gang's still lookin' for your Joey at the top of the Steps."

"Well, yer have ter live dangerously sometimes," said Rocky. "See youse den."

After he had left, the Cats sat in silence for some minutes, feeling guilty and troubled.

93

"Should have told Rocky the truth about that shop," said Billy.

"He wouldn't have believed us – got it into his head it's jewellery," said Beady.

"It will be all right," said Little Chan. "There is certainly something in that shop – and it is better for Rocky and us if it is not jewellery."

The Cats were all in place that morning and Rocky was standing on the pavement in Larkspur Lane, beside the parked car from which the man had just removed a box and taken it into the shop. Rocky was just about to look into what might be in the boot when a man rushed past and dropped a plastic bag at his feet.

"Keep dat for me, will yer," he said, and ran off.

He was followed almost immediately by Constable McMahon, who panted, "Did you see a man running this way?"

"Yes."

"Where'd he go?"

"Straight on ter your place – maybe givin' himself up."

Constable McMahon ran on, talking into his radio.

"What's goin' on, Rocky?" Beady shouted.

"Don't know yet, but I think the job's off for today. Will yer tell the Cats?" And Rocky picked up the plastic bag.

"But we've been hangin' about," protested Beady.

"So've I, but we've had other events, haven't we? Like this," and he held up the plastic bag.

But Rocky hadn't time to investigate the plastic bag before a police car, a jam-butty, pulled up and an officer got out, talking into his radio, and then said, "Right, what's this?" indicating the bag. "Let's have it."

"Don't know," said Rocky, leaning back against the wall, relaxed. "Was just dropped at me feet."

"Heard that one before, son. The handbag in here was just snatched from an old lady in Joseph Terrace."

"Well," said Rocky, "dat's not new, is it? Dey're always snatchin' . . ."

"Come on. Into the car. You'll have to be questioned."

"Yer from der cons' place in Larkspur?"

"Come *on!*"

"Well, it's just dat I'd rather do Larkspur – dey know me, see? I caught a big criminal for dem. Dey owe me . . ."

In the police station the sergeant looked surprised at seeing Rocky in the charge of another policeman carrying a plastic bag.

"Not done Lewis's, have yer, Rocky?" he asked.

"Not done nobody. Was just dropped at me feet."

"The handbag in here," said the arresting officer, "was snatched from an old lady in Joseph Terrace fifteen minutes ago. It contains her savings of a thousand pounds. It was found in the possession of this boy."

The sergeant looked puzzled. "Yer did her, Rocky?"

"Haven't done nobody. It was dis feller. Just done me paper round and waiting for me mates when dis feller ran past an' dropped dis at me feet an' said would I keep it for him. Now, dat's put me in a difficult position, see. If dat feller comes

95

back he's goin' ter think I've shopped him ter you lot, in't he? An' he'll do me. So I'll need police protection."

"Was it a boy did the old lady?" the sergeant asked the arresting officer. "Did she say it was a boy?"

"No, but . . ."

"Have yer got McMahon around?" asked Rocky. "He was chasin' the man that dropped the bag. He can clear me."

McMahon appeared, looking hot and angry.

"This business of the snatched handbag," said the sergeant. "Do you know who did it?"

"Yes, and I've got a description but he got away . . ."

"Wasn't Rocky did it?"

"Rocky? No. Why d'yer think . . . ?"

"Because he claims this was dropped at his feet," said the sergeant, holding up the plastic bag with the handbag in it.

"No. The snatcher had that – that's why I was after him. Well," he added, rather doubtfully, "Rocky *did* see him running past – and he told me the direction he took."

"He's an accomplice," suggested the arresting officer. "It was all set up. This boy was waiting for him."

"Yer wrong," said McMahon. "The snatcher couldn't have known he needed Rocky. He couldn't have known I would be there when he snatched the handbag."

"Dat's brill," said Rocky, admiring and relieved. "Real brill."

"That's enough from you," said the sergeant. "This is a serious matter. Now, Rocky's not a

96

good lad, but he wouldn't snatch an old lady's handbag. If he says it was dropped at his feet, it was dropped at his feet. Yer'll have to go back on things. Must be somebody in Joseph's knew the villain – he must have sussed the place. And, Rocky, I'm sick of having you around here once every week, so get off and I don't want ter see yer for another fortnight."

"Thanks very much for clearin' me," said Rocky. "Could of lost me paper round, if yer hadn't. Terra, well. See youse." And he left the station.

The Cats were waiting anxiously outside Pa Richardson's.

"What happened, Rocky?" asked Billy. "Did dey find yer with . . ."

"Feller come past an' dropped a stolen handbag at me feet – from Joseph's. Cons took me in, but McMahon cleared me."

"Better give this one up, Rocky. The police'll be active," said Billy. "Think about it."

"Notice you lot disappeared quick," said Rocky.

"Yer never gettin' this one done," said the Nabber.

"I'll gerrit done. Show yer!"

Billy, Little Chan and Beady looked dubious but said nothing.

"Better gerron," said Beady, and they started along Larkspur Lane, followed by the Nabber, chewing something and relaxed.

"Nutter," he commented.

"Show youse!" shouted Rocky.

Then Mr Oliver came out of the newsagent's.

"Want a word with yer, Rocky," he said, very seriously.

"What's it?"

"Was speakin' ter Mr Richardson – 'bout you."

"Done nothin'."

"He was sorry for Suzie and give her chocolates, dat right?"

"Well, he did."

"An' then *you* go an' make a scene in his shop complainin' about pizzas . . ."

"But dey were . . ."

"Dey weren't, an' you know it. Go an' apologize, Rocky, or I'm finished wid you, an' I'll not give yer help for a job again."

Rocky had not seen the wingy as angry as that before, but he was angry himself, what with everything, and was inclined to say, "Right. Suit yerself." But then he thought about it.

"All right," he said. "Yer gorra point. I'll see him."

Pa Richardson took a step back behind the counter as Rocky came into the shop. "What yer want?" he asked.

"Don't want nothin'. Come ter apologize 'bout der pizzas. Wasn't on, not after what yer give Suzie."

Pa Richardson relaxed. "Well (sniff), not der way (sniff) ter go on."

"Yer right."

"Well, thanks for comin' in. How's she, yer sister?"

"Gettin' on. Not over it, but. Still don't know who did it." And Pa Richardson felt Rocky's anxiety.

Outside the shop, Rocky hunched his

shoulders, pushed his hands into his pockets and followed the Cats, who were far ahead of him. Finish with them, he thought. They don't appreciate what's done for them, and he considered joining the Bone-Breakers. He got on well with Blair Turner and he could maybe make his way and take over from him. And their football team was good. The thought cheered him up, and at morning break he very ostentatiously went to talk to Blair and one or two of the Bone-Breakers as an opening move and came away very satisfied. He avoided the Cats and enjoyed their obvious concern, though the Nabber remained deliberately relaxed and detached.

"Show them," Rocky thought.

At the top of the Steps he hesitated. Murky Evans and *all* the Crown Street Gang were assembled and looked prepared for a siege. Rocky hoped to get past them without trouble but Murky grabbed him.

"I don't know where ..." Rocky began, but Murky cut in.

"*We* know where, but – in there," and he pointed to Number 3. "Tell him we'll be here when he comes out."

"Tell him," said Rocky, wondering where Murky had got the information about Joey's decision to return. "How'd yer know he was comin', but?"

"I've got international contacts."

Rocky didn't believe it. Murky didn't look as if he had contacts outside Liverpool 8, nor maybe even outside Crown Street, but it could be that he had contacts with one of Joey's friends locally.

Maybe one who helped Joey with the Ratman's loot, didn't get the cut he expected and shopped Joey to Murky when he knew Joey was coming back. Was a dangerous situation, Rocky thought. You couldn't know what the Crown Street Gang would do next – maybe come storming into Number 3 and drag Joey out. Then he thought they could follow *him* now and push into Number 3 after him. He started running.

"Hi!" Murky shouted after him. "Got information for yer!"

"Have ter keep!" Rocky shouted back.

In the living room of Number 3 there was a lot of cigarette smoke. Joey was sitting beside the electric fire with his feet on the stool, a glass of beer in his hand and looking worried. His mother was sitting opposite with a cup of tea, looking happy, though the happiness changed to annoyance when Rocky rushed in and slammed the door and locked it.

"What's up wid *you*? Practisin' for der Derby?" his mother asked. "Joey's back."

"Can see dat."

"An' he's brought dat bottle of red wine."

"My favourite bevvy," said Rocky, looking at the bottle on the table. "Must of cost a lot," he added sarcastically, and dropped on to the sofa behind the table. "What yer back for, but? What's wrong wid Spain? Thought it was great."

Joey tried to sound superior. "Yer can have too much sun," he said.

"Suppose yer could have too much of the Spanish scuffers as well. What *dey* gorron yer?"

"Got nothin' on me."

"Well," said Rocky reasonably, "yer can have

too much of der Crown Street Gang an' Murky Evans as well. Dey're waitin' for yer out der. Yer seen dem?"

Joey snapped, "I've seen dem. Couldn't miss dem, could I?"

"Dey'll not miss *you*."

"What yer both on about?" asked Mrs Flanagan desperately.

"Joey knows."

But Joey said nothing. He lit another cigarette.

"Wur's Suzie, but?" asked Rocky.

"Be in der school," said his mother.

"No, she'll not be. Not this time. Did she not come back?"

"Well," said Mrs Flanagan, vaguely, "she was here when Joey come."

"Well, did she go out?"

"Didn't see her go out."

"Must of gone. She's taken off. Have ter go an' find her," and Rocky went out, thinking of the places Suzie might have gone to hide in because Joey was back.

She wasn't in the abandoned car or the builder's hut in the disused garden. He went all round the bone orchard behind the Anglican Cathedral, shouting for her, because she'd often hidden among the tombstones there, but he couldn't find her. She wasn't in the bus shelter on Prinney Boulevard, or the shelter in Prinney Park or the one in Seffy Park. She wasn't in the ruins of the Ratman's house. He couldn't think of any other place she would have known about. But she could have gone downtown by herself and he couldn't handle that one. Have to get the cons on to it, he decided, and started running. Had to get something done quick. It was getting dark.

As he passed Murky Evans at the top of the Steps, Murky grabbed him.

"Joey know the score?" he asked.

"Listen, I'm lookin' for me sister who's lost an' I couldn't care less about our Joey!" shouted Rocky.

"Told yer, but," said Murky, letting him go. "Had information for yer."

"Got ter get der cons lookin' for Suzie!"

"Yer sister? Hi, Fosser," he shouted to one of his gang, "dat incident yer saw . . ."

Fosser came over. He was tall, looked vacant and had ears so big you wouldn't be surprised if he took off in a high wind.

"Startin' the attack now, Murky?" he asked.

"Put a trap on yer moey, will yer, Fosser?" requested Murky. "Yer could make a good livin' as a town crier! Dat's confidential information regardin' our plans for a certain person. No. Dis feller wants ter know about his sister – young kid, beaten up – what yer *saw*."

"Oh, dat – Prinney Boulevard? Well, it was just an incident. Der was some shoutin' an' screamin' an' I couldn't see what was goin' on – der was a car in the way, then it went off and some people went into a house."

"What yer mean – people?"

"Well, der was a man an' a woman an' a young girl or maybe boy."

"Know which house?"

"Well, just one of dem on Prinney Boulevard."

"Well," said Rocky, "I've heard about dat incident. Doesn't help."

"What else did yer see?" Murky demanded. "Think about it, Fosser."

Fosser thought, and then said, "Der was an old woman in a long black coat walkin' along."

"Thanks, Fosser," said Rocky, and started off for Princes Boulevard.

"What about Joey?" shouted Murky.

"Your problem," Rocky shouted back.

Suzie was sitting on the low wall that surrounded the fill-in garden next to the weird house, with the old woman in the long black coat. They were both eating crisps in the light of the street lamp.

"What yer doin', tatty-'ead? What yer up to?" Rocky demanded. "Yer've had me worried."

"Good, Rocky," said Suzie, offering him a crisp. "An' him bad."

"I know yer mean Joey, but he'll not stay long. Thanks for lookin' after her, missus," he said to the old woman. Her white hair was so thin, you could see the pink scalp underneath shimmer. Her eyes, looking out from a small, monkey-like face, were never still, looking one way and another without seeming to take anything in.

"She needs lookin' after in this place. She can't look after herself. Can yer, Suzie?"

"How'd yer get to know her, but? She generally doesn't bother wid people."

"Oh, we got to saying 'hello' when she was comin' and goin' ter school."

"Well, missus, yer might have seen somethin'. Few days back. Did yer see a incident round here – car an' a man an' a woman an' a girl an' shoutin'?"

The old woman's eyes were still for a few seconds, fixed on him, then they moved again.

"I never see nothin'. Better not to."

"But look, missus, it's about Suzie. Somebody mugged her around here – yer can see from her face! She was battered!"

"Never seen nothin'. Better take her home."

"Not go!" shouted Suzie.

"Yer have to, luv," said the old woman. "Yer can always come back."

Suzie thought about it, then nodded. "Come back," she said, and went along the Boulevard with Rocky, shouting, "Good! Good!"

"Will yer shurrup, Suzie! Makin' an exhibition of yerself. Dey'll have yer in a pantomime yet!"

That was the "good" woman all right, but why was she so afraid? And why did Suzie draw her like a coffin?

Murky Evans let them pass without any bother, though he and his gang showed no sign of moving.

"Listen, Murky," Rocky said to him, rubbing his hands through his red hair, "we can't go on livin' like dis! Yer'll have ter clear off!"

Murky fixed him with his brown eyes. "When your Joey comes out. Glad yer got *her* back."

John was right, Rocky thought. Murky *did* have a good side – sometimes.

"Rocky." It was Mr Oliver, just coming out of the house at the end of the Square. He closed the garden gate carefully. "Can yer not get rid of that lot?" He nodded at Murky's gang. "Proper menace."

"Can't do nothin', Mr Oliver. McMahon can't do nothin'. They want Joey."

Mr Oliver became thoughtful. "Have ter get Joey out privately," he decided.

"Yer mean some time about midnight?"

"Somethin' like that."

"Gorranother problem, Mr Oliver . . ." He was thinking of the girl in that house.

"Sorry, Rocky. Have ter wait. Wife's shoutin'. Wants ter be taken out." And Mr Oliver retreated into the house.

Best thing, Rocky reflected, was not have a brother or a stepfather or a – "Oh, come on, tatty-'ead!" he shouted.

Suzie looked up at him seriously. "Old woman good," she said.

"I know, but yer gettin' ter be monotonous."

It was very peaceful in Number 3. Mrs Flanagan was asleep in her chair, and Joey was asleep in his.

"Dead," whispered Suzie hopefully. "All dead."

"Don't be holler-headed, tatty-'ead. Dey're just sleepin'. Come on – yer can sleep in Joey's bed ternight. Don't think he'll want it."

As he lay listening to Suzie muttering in her sleep, he made up his mind. He didn't want to upset her any more, but in spite of what the old woman had said he was sure that what had happened to Suzie had happened near her garden and the weird house. Tomorrow, he would take Suzie with him on his paper round. Maybe at that time in the morning when everything looked a bit sinister, it would take Suzie's mind back.

CHAPTER

9

Next morning, Rocky wakened Suzie quietly.

"Right, tatty-'ead," he said. "Doin' der paper round wid me?"

Suzie sat up and rubbed her eyes. "Do yer round," she said.

"Have ter keep yer eyes open for things, but. Norra trip round Prinney Park."

"Keep eyes open?"

"Ter see if yer recognize where yer were beaten up."

Suzie shrank back. "Bad!" she said.

"I know it was . . ."

"Old woman good."

"Tatty-'ead, yer mind gettin' yerself up an' dressed. Got me paper round ter do!"

At the newsagent's shop, Rocky stopped and said to Suzie, "You stay here – just till I get me bag."

"Come wid yer," said Suzie, looking at what was going on inside which seemed interesting.

"Told yer. Stay here. An' dat's important. Got it?"

"Got it," said Suzie, but went up close to the window to see what was happening.

"All right, Rocky?" asked Blair, handing him his bag.

"All right. How's Joseph's?"

"Far as I know, quiet. Somethin' wrong wid you?"

Rocky shouldered his bag. "Me? Never nothin' wrong wid me! See yer!"

Suzie followed him along Joseph Terrace and up and down the staircases, muttering "Chick's Lot" fiercely, because she didn't forget the fights the Cats and Chick's Lot had had on the waste ground behind the old houses.

"Chick's Lot's not up yet," said Rocky. "Keep up wid me, tatty-'ead, or yer'll lose yerself."

She didn't show any more interest in anything and Rocky began to think he was wasting his time taking her around, but when they got to the weird house on Princes Boulevard, Suzie stopped at the gate.

"All right, tatty-'ead. Come on, an' I'll let yer put the paper in."

But Suzie didn't move. She stood glaring at the house and muttering, "Bad, swine. Bad, swine." And suddenly she shouted, "Swine! Not go der, Rocky!"

Rocky went back to her anxiously. "Come on, Suzie. What's der matter?" He was really worried by her reaction. She looked ready to take off. He rushed back to the door and pushed in the paper, and Suzie was beside him, staring at the door.

"Come on, tatty-'ead," he said, turning away.

But Suzie said, "Wait, Rocky."

"What's it, but?"

"Paper gone."

"Course it has. What's new. Come on . . ."

Then the flap of the letter-box was pulled back and the girl's voice said again, but more desperately, "Help, *please* help me!"

"Bad!" shouted Suzie.

"Shurrup, will yer?" He bent down to the letter box. "What yer need help for, but?"

"Kidnapped. Kidnapped. Please let my father know. Please."

"Who's yer father?"

"Rahman. Yusof Rahman."

"Wur's he?"

"London. He is our country's ambassador there. I give you his phone number. Please phone him!" she replied desperately.

"Wur's the woman that lives here?"

"Gone out, but she'll be back. Please help quickly."

Rocky considered. Phoning was no good – might be no answer.

"Here, will yer stop all this noise?" It was the old lady in the long coat. She was crawling out of the long cardboard box in the garden next door. "I don't get up this early. Too cold. Go away." And she started to crawl back.

And then Rocky understood it all. The coffin was a cardboard box, the old lady good, the blonde woman in the weird house bad. This was where Suzie had been beaten up, and the woman and the man must have done it – *and* kidnapped the girl.

"Hi, missus!" Rocky shouted at the cardboard box. "Can yer come out a minute?"

The grey head reappeared, "What yer want now? I told yer . . ."

"Need yer help. See, der's a girl in there, been kidnapped an' I think yer saw dem take her in, an' I think me sister here must have seen it happen and tried ter stop it an' got knocked about, an' you must have helped her . . ."

"You from der police?"

"Me? Yer coddin'!"

"Social Security?"

"Listen, missus . . ."

"Not goin' inter a home."

"Listen, will yer! I just deliver papers. But I have ter do somethin' about this girl. She says the woman's gone out, so I can maybe get her out."

The old woman thought about it, and then crawled out of the box and leant on her supermarket trolley. "Have ter be careful," she said. "Put yer in a home if yer not careful. Yer'll never get in there, inter that house."

Rocky thought desperately, while the girl kept begging for help. Suzie shouted, "Bad!" and started to look for a suitable half-brick.

"All right, Suzie, I know what yer on about now. Listen. Der Cats'll be in Larkspur. Can yer go an' get them. Say it's urgent. Bring dem here – an' a half-brick as well if yer can find one."

Suzie nodded and ran off.

"If yer ever have any spare, I could use them," said the old woman.

"Any what spare?"

"Newspapers. Keep yer warm."

Rocky bent down to the letter-box. "How long'll she be away?"

"About an hour, but she's been away about half an hour."

It was urgent, all right, Rocky thought. But what could he do?

"Can yer not open der door?"

"She took the key."

"Back door?"

"That also."

"Can yer get into the front room here?"

"Yes. I am always in there."

"Can yer open der window?"

"It also is locked. Please . . ."

"Well, is der anythin' yer can break the window wid?"

"No – there's nothing." The girl sobbed. "You cannot help! Please phone my father . . ."

Couldn't wait for the Cats, he decided. "Listen, stay where you are till I tell yer ter move. And keep away from the front window!" He started looking for a missile. There were one or two large stones, but nothing that would make a real impression.

Then the old woman asked, "Are you finished with dem papers?"

"Probably will be," said Rocky. "For good. Want ter break this window. Got a good big stone or a piece of cement? Yer must have somethin' in that trolley."

"Just a minute," said the old woman. She rummaged in the trolley and came up with a large hammer. "Found it on a tip," she said proudly. "Very useful, that. *Was* yer sister them next door knocked about when she tried ter get that girl away from them. Put up a good fight for her size. I pulled her in here – tried ter calm her down."

"Thanks, missus." Rocky put down his bag of papers, grabbed the hammer, took off his anorak and pulled it over his head, went to the window, stretched up as far as he could, held the hammer back and then hit the window as hard as he could. There was a terrific crash and glass fell around him. He got back quickly and watched as almost the whole of the window that hadn't been shattered slid down. And there was an even more enormous crash.

When he turned round and pulled off his anorak he saw a large number of pedestrians watching in amazement and three cars run into one another because of the drivers' shock. Suzie and the Cats were running towards the house, Billy on his tricycle, and each of them carrying a brick.

"Good, Rocky!" Suzie shouted.

"Yer all right, Rocky?" asked Billy.

"Never seen nothin' like it!" exclaimed Beady.

"One of yer best," the Nabber admitted admiringly.

"How can she get out over all that glass?" asked Little Chan, indicating the little girl, who was crying and shaking and had come to the window. "Better get the police."

Rocky ran down the path to the stationary cars. "Any of youse gorra car phone?" he asked.

"I have," said one man. "But what's happened?"

"Will yer get the police?"

"Hi," hissed the old woman as he went back to the house, "want me hammer back – now. Dey'll take it in evidence."

Rocky handed it over.

"And der papers?"

Rocky considered the matter and concluded that he wouldn't be delivering them anyway, and that his career as a newspaper deliverer was probably finished.

"Here yer are," and he tipped them out of the bag and into her supermarket trolley. "Der's a library for yer as well as blankets."

"You mind yer lip. Goin' ter have ter move

again because of you. Dey'll investigate." And she started packing her trolley.

Then she stopped. "There was a feller as well as the blonde woman – dark-haired and dark-skinned. That's all I know, and I didn't tell yer nothin', remember."

Suzie pulled at his anorak. "Good, Rocky, but," she said.

"Not always, tatty-'ead," he said. "I'll be down in the police station again now."

And he was. He was taken there in a police car, while the kidnapped girl was taken away in an ambulance. The old woman had disappeared into her box as soon as the police arrived, and Rocky hastily asked the Cats to see that Suzie got home safely.

Suzie scowled. "Not go," she said. "Go wid *you*."

"Yer can't, tatty-'ead. Yer have ter go wid der Cats, see? I've got things ter see to. An' if yer behave yerself, I'll bring yer somethin' back."

"Beastly Wobblies . . ."

"Wait an' see! If yer don't behave yerself, yer'll get nothin'. Got it?"

Suzie nodded. "Go wid *dem*," she confirmed.

"If me mam's norr'in, take her up ter Ellen, or see Mr Oliver."

"Don't worry, Rocky. We'll see she's all right," said Beady. "Yer goin' ter give evidence?"

"That'll be it. Well, I've done nothin' wrong, have I?"

"No," said the Nabber encouragingly. "I mean, smashin' a window like that's nothin'. Is it?"

"Do you, Nabber Neville!"

"Yer coming, Rocky?" asked the policeman.

"Gorra choice, have I?" He got into the car, sitting in the back. They started off, and Rocky began to enjoy it. It was a new experience. He dropped his sack on the floor and sat back.

"Hi, what about de siren?" he asked.

"Don't need that."

"Well, I thought I'd get a siren. At least!"

The driver smiled. "All right. Yer can have it."

As it wailed, Rocky felt totally happy, even though it didn't go on for long. It wasn't far to Larkspur Lane police station, but they drew up there with the siren still going. The door was opened for him and he stepped out with his newspaper sack, feeling and trying (unsuccessfully) to look like the Prince of Wales.

Rocky walked confidently into the police station. This time he had a lot of expectations. The desk sergeant, looking slightly bewildered, welcomed him.

"'Lo den, wack," Rocky greeted him. "Wur's de fella in charge? Gorra lot ter tell him. An' if I'm goin' ter be long, yer better let me mam know."

"We'll see to that." The sergeant took him into the interview room and provided him with a WPC, a detective who Rocky suspected was not run-of-the-mill, a cup of tea and a digestive biscuit. He was built like a tank, was the detective, and he had a round head, bullet-proof, Rocky reflected. When Rocky sat down he moved slowly forward a few inches across the desk, fixing Rocky with blank eyes. Rocky was not impressed. The scuffers had nothing on him this time.

"I'm not bein' charged with nothin', and I'm not payin' for dat window," he announced.

The tank retreated a few inches.

"Just tell us what you know about the incident in Princes Boulevard."

"All right, wack. It'll interest yer." He told the detective everything that had happened, starting with Suzie's being beaten up.

"Yer see, like, only thing I could do," he finished, "was smash der window. She all right – the girl?"

"Just shocked." The detective moved forward a few inches. "You say that a man and a woman were involved. Can you describe them?"

"Well, the woman was blonde – long hair – like Ellen-from-upstairs."

"Like who?"

"Well, yer wuddent know her, but you can ask the sergeant – *he* knows her. An' I was told the man was dark-skinned, but I never seen him, but the newsagents in Larkspur could tell yer – he must have ordered the papers from dem."

The detective moved forward again rather threateningly across the desk.

"Have you any evidence about the incident with the car and the man, woman and girl? Any witnesses?"

Rocky moved slightly back in *his* chair. "Well, I wouldn't have, would I? I wasn't der. But I asked around. Yer see, I'm certain dat my stepsister, Suzie, was comin' back from school an' saw what was happenin' and tried ter help the girl – she's like dat, is Suzie – an' she got badly beaten up by der woman."

"Witnesses?" the detective insisted.

Rocky was beginning to feel less sure of things. He said nothing about the old woman in the cardboard box, but he told the detective about Suzie's drawings and her fear of the house, and he told him about Betty Mulloney and Fosser. "The sergeant knows about Betty – he'll tell yer," he said in a conciliatory way.

The detective moved forward another inch. "Who's Fosser?"

"Not sure," said Rocky quickly. "Just a feller lives around der – don't know wur, but. But he saw it happen."

The tank regarded him silently, and Rocky felt definitely uneasy. Then he said, "You've been helpful – very. Though we still need witnesses and more evidence. *But* what you've told us supports our ideas of who the kidnappers could be, so I'll tell you, in strict confidence, what the situation is."

Rocky relaxed slightly, though he was still wary. "Thanks very much."

"A few weeks ago the girl was kidnapped and demands for money came in. She is the daughter of an ambassador . . ."

"Dat's right," said Rocky brightly.

"How do you know that?"

"Well, she told me, didn't she? She wanted me to phone him!" Proper nit, this one, he thought.

"The ambassador is a wealthy and important man – a good target for kidnappers, especially if they came from his country. But you must not say anything about this yet. Nothing must get out that might alert the two we're looking for. The ambassador and his family are constantly guarded but they won't be safe until we've got the kidnappers. Understand?"

"Well, yes – I'm norra holler head! But what about – der's me mam – she'll want ter know

where I've been. An' der's me gang's mams –
dey'll want ter know . . ."

"Just say, you *and* your gang, you witnessed an
accident – you saw the cars pile up on Princes
Boulevard and you had to give us your evidence.
That's all."

"Well, but," Rocky began to protest. It didn't
seem fair – he'd done all that and it came down
to a traffic accident! "Here – what about me stepsister? Dat woman mugged her bad. She should
be sent to prison for it!"

The tank reflected. "Of course, when we have
evidence. But what will have to be taken into
account is whether it would be right to put your
sister through the ordeal of going over that again
some time after it happened. It would upset her,
wouldn't it?"

Rocky knew it would. And he thought again.

"But the reward? What about that?" he asked
hopefully.

"I know nothing about that. None was offered.
Everything had to be kept under wraps – and still
has. Understand?" He retreated across the desk.
"Thanks for co-operating. I expect something will
come your way . . ."

"Co-operatin'!" Rocky was disgusted. "Never
trust a scuffer!" He left the room.

Outside he faced the desk sergeant. "I'll want
notes for Little Chan, Beady Martin, Nabber
Neville and Billy Griffiths to say why we didn't
get ter school," he snapped.

The sergeant said he would see that the school
was contacted.

"Thanks very much."

"What's the matter?"

"Nothin's the matter!"

"Rocky, yer could have reported this business to us instead of taking it into yer own hands . . ."

"There wasn't time!"

"But I have to say that what you did, you did spectacularly."

Rocky was slightly mollified.

"Thanks very much."

"So – don't mess it up by talking about it." The sergeant picked up the phone and asked for a call to the headmaster of Rocky's school.

Rocky stalked out. Think there'd be a reward at least!

Joey was an island in a sea of chaos as he sat by the electric fire in the living room of Number 3 St Catherine's Square, with his feet on the stool and his face in the pages of the *Liverpool Echo*. There was chaos, created by Mrs Flanagan, who had embarked on some house cleaning. The carpet was rolled back, the sofa pushed against the wall, and a small cloud of dust went ahead of her brush. She looked round at Rocky.

"Had the police here about you," she said. "What yer been up to now?"

"They would of told yer – saw a accident."

"Well, yer shouldn't of! Her from next door would have seen the police, an' it'll be all round der Square! An' yer'll have ter keep out of my way."

"Dey're still waitin' for yer out there. Seen dem?" Rocky said.

Joey snapped, "Yeah, yeah, mind yer business."

"When is one of youse goin' to tell me what dis

is all about?" asked Mrs Flanagan knowing she wouldn't get an answer.

"Wur's Suzie, but?" Rocky asked. "Did the gang not bring her back?"

"She's here somewhere – behind the table."

"No space – she's run off," said Rocky, but this time he knew where to find her.

She was sitting in the garden of the house on Princes Boulevard, eating a sandwich and watching the old woman pack her possessions into the supermarket trolley, and the policeman on duty outside the house next door with its front door and window now boarded up.

"Yer should have stayed at home, Suzie. Come on," he said.

"Stay wid her. Happy here."

"She's a quaint one, but she put up a good fight. You take her with you," said the old woman, buttoning up her long black coat. "She'll forget me. Have they got the man and the blonde woman?"

"Don't know yet, but the girl's safe anyway."

"I'm movin' on. Found a place in Lodge Lane. Not safe here now that the cons have been round." She looked up at the house and said, "Had a flat der once, but dey did me three times and made messes yer could hardly bring yerself to clean up, an' I always kept a clean house. So I give it up and camped out. S'better. Terra well." She went off, pushing her trolley down Princes Boulevard in the direction of Lodge Lane.

"Come on, tatty-'ead," said Rocky. "Yer comin' back, an' yer can finish yer sandwich on der way."

Suzie followed, eating her sandwich and shouting at intervals in an upset voice, "Woman in box good!"

In Number 3 St Catherine's Square, the activity was over, and Mrs Flanagan was slumped in her chair. Seeing Joey, Suzie hid behind the sofa. "Dey still out der? Crown Street?" asked Joey.

"Dey'll move when the pubs open," said Rocky, "but they'll leave somebody on duty like the cons do."

"An' wur did yer find *her*?" asked Mrs Flanagan. "She'll have ter stop this runnin' off. I'm not havin' any more of it. She'll have ter see the social worker!"

Suzie frowned and began chuntering angrily.

"Anythin' ter eat, mam?" asked Rocky hastily. "Had nothin' since I went out this mornin'."

"An' dat's another thing," said Mrs Flanagan suddenly. "What yer out for every mornin' early? What yer doin'? Not just exercise. Can't be. I'll have a word wid Mr Oliver about it."

"Well," said Rocky, "der's no harm in that." For he wasn't likely to be welcomed back by the newsagents since he'd given away all those newspapers. He could, however, collect what pay was still due to him.

"Joey," said Mrs Flanagan, "I want ter know what's goin' on."

Joey stubbed out his cigarette and lit another one. "Can't tell yer yet. Be all right."

Rocky pulled Suzie out from behind the sofa. "Come on, tatty-'ead. Chans'll be open, just."

"Wur yer goin' now?" demanded Mrs Flanagan.

"Out," said Rocky.

At the top of the Steps, one of Murky's gang

stopped them. "Wur's your Joey? Murky wants ter know," he said.

"Joey's in Number 3, an' Murky knows it. See yer," and he ran down the Steps, followed by Suzie, who occasionally sobbed and muttered, "Woman in box good."

"Wouldn't give yer fish an' chips, but."

"Would!"

"Wouldn't!"

They didn't make a very good impression when they went into the newsagent's, what with Rocky producing his empty paper sack and Suzie glowering and muttering. The pair behind the counter looked at them, one sternly, the other disappointed.

"Come ter hand me bag in," said Rocky.

"You're very late," said the man with the granny bicycles.

"Lot's been happenin', and I'm turnin' in the job before yer ask me to."

"*What's* been happenin'?" asked the woman.

"A lot," said Rocky, "an' I didn't deliver all along Prinney Boulevard because of everythin', so I give the rest of the papers away to a deservin' cause, so yer'll expect me ter give the job up, but I'll want me pay up to today, including the fact that I did most of the drops dis mornin'."

"Don't know about that," said the woman. "You've been very irresponsible."

"Yer owe me for the days I done, an' I want der money for dem," said Rocky, getting angry. "An' yer got yer bag back an' dat's somethin' . . ."

The bell on the shop door rang and Blair Turner came in, breathless.

"Hi, Rocky. Yer all right? Heard what happened. Heard der glass smashin'. Who did it?"

"Me," said Rocky. "Had to."

"Yer mean yer made all that mess at that house?"

"Yes," said Rocky. "An' in similar circumstances, would do it again."

"What yer mean, circumstances? What kind of, but?"

"Can't tell yer," said Rocky, getting into his stride. "Top secret, see? Been sworn ter secrecy. Anyway, just come in for me money an' that's me finished, but the match is on, in't it? An' listen," he said to the couple behind the counter, "dat round of drops is der most dangerous, an' I _know_ the area. Yer'd better get a con to deliver there. An' can I have der money due ter me?"

The couple went into consultation and came up with what Rocky considered a ridiculous amount, even taking into account the loss of the newspapers which he couldn't be expected to have delivered, given the morning's events. They were all arguing over it and Suzie had just found a missile in the shape of a fairly hefty copy of _Good Housekeeping_, when the wingy came in and paused for a moment to consider the situation.

"What's it?" he asked.

"I've given it up, der round," said Rocky, "but dey won't pay me for what I done."

"He's thrown away a lot of copies," said the woman.

"I didn't. I give them away in a good cause."

"Shurrup, will yer, Rocky? I'll do some explainin'. Had a word with Mac." And Mr Oliver went into whispered consultation with the couple behind the counter, with many backward glances from all three at Rocky and Suzie, who was still considering the impact of *Good Housekeeping*, and who still had a bruised face and a rather purple eye which did not add to her credibility.

"What yer do it for, Rocky?" Blair repeated. "I mean – yer must be mad."

"Yer don't know nothin'," retorted Rocky. "An' whatever happens, I'm having me free comic."

The consultation at the counter ended, and Mr Oliver turned and put his hand on Rocky's shoulder. "All right, Rocky. We've got it settled. All right? That suit yer?"

"What's der terms?" asked Rocky belligerently.

"You can keep the job, Rocky," said the woman behind the counter, "and we'll pay you a bonus for danger."

"How much?"

"We'll have ter go inter that," said Mr Oliver, "but in the meantime the job's all right and yer've got yer comic . . ."

Rocky pushed his hand through his red hair, making it stand on end. "Know what it is – free publicity! When the story breaks yer'll have everybody in buying papers!"

"What's der story, but?" asked Blair.

"Now, Rocky, we'll leave it at that. An' Saturday morning's der match. All right?" interrupted Mr Oliver.

Rocky calmed down and pocketed the comic. "All right," he said. "An' dis is the feller that runs der Bone-Breakers."

"Pleased ter meet yer," said Mr Oliver.

"An' you," said the leader of the Bone-Breakers.

"Right," said Mr Oliver, sounding tired.

Rocky rescued *Good Housekeeping* from Suzie, and they walked along to Chan's with Mr Oliver.

"Yer'll be feeling a bit down after all the excitement."

Rocky shrugged.

"An' havin' ter keep quiet, according to Mac?"

"Can do *that*. Can put a trap on me moey."

"Well listen, Rocky, it'll come out all right. Yer'll see. When the story breaks yer mug'll be on the front page of every newspaper. Yer'll see!"

"Think so?"

"Sure of it."

Rocky grinned. "Thanks, Mr Oliver."

"Need a handout?" Mr Oliver asked.

"No – thanks. Got enough."

"And if yer need any help . . ."

"Know wur to come. An' thanks, Mr Oliver."

"Saturday den?"

"Dat's right." And he went to get the fish and chips.

But as they went into the chippy, he felt depressed and annoyed – after all, he'd rescued that girl, found out Suzie's mugger, and put the scuffers on to the track of the kidnappers – and what did he get? Nothing. Just keep your mouth shut.

Well, he thought, I'll show them. There's still that jewellery shop. I'll *show* them!

CHAPTER

10

It took a lot of persuasion to get the Cats to agree to do the job on Larkspur Lane, and it bothered Rocky that all his talk of the jewellery didn't make much difference, but at last Beady said, "All right, *I'll* go for it," and then Billy agreed reluctantly, and then the others. Though the Nabber remained absolutely disinterested in the whole thing, he didn't say he wouldn't take part.

"Must be a jinx on you," he said as they went down the Steps to Larkspur Lane.

"What yer mean, jinx?"

"Well, all this business of smashin' windows – wur's de point? We have to keep quiet and der's not a mention in the papers."

"Yer ignorant, Nabber Neville. Yer don't understand nothin'. Anyway, what did *you* do? Did nothin'. An' all yer've been asked ter do is shurrup. So shurrup! Now der plan's same as before . . ."

"Same failure," the Nabber muttered.

Rocky ignored him. "Billy and Little Chan keeping dowse, Beady ready ter run an' Mr Knowall and Do Nothin' on the Steps."

"Are you sure we should do this again, Rocky?" asked Little Chan, whose conscience was troubling him.

"'Course I'm sure! It's dead easy, an' we'll make a bomb! Get in yer places. He'll be comin'.'"

Doubtfully the Cats dispersed, and Rocky leant against the wall innocently, gazing into space, but he was aware when the car was approaching, and he became tense. He'd show the Cats this time.

It went like clockwork. Billy and Little Chan hooted like owls, the man opened the boot and went into the shop. Rocky snatched a package from the boot and threw it to Beady who ran with it to the Nabber who ran with it up the Steps and into the hideout. The rest of the Cats sauntered towards the Steps, helping Billy up with his tricycle.

The Nabber put the parcel on the card table. "This all yer got?" he asked. "After all that organization? Not cost effective."

"Don't know what's in it, but," said Beady.

"Not a lot unless it's jewellery," said Little Chan.

"Well, it's very light an' it's soft," contributed the Nabber. "Funny jewellery!" He grinned at the others, but the Cats didn't respond. They were anxious.

"It'll be well packed," said Rocky. "Jewellery always is," and excitedly he began to open the parcel.

"Could be a bomb, Rocky," warned Billy.

It wasn't. It was rolls of cotton wool!

"Can't unload that in Joseph's," said the Nabber, and the Cats couldn't keep back the laughter any longer.

"Lewis's Santa Claus at Christmas," gasped Beady.

"Soft toys," contributed Little Chan.

Rocky sat frowning down at the old card table and thinking back to the workmen in that shop. He'd been conned, and he was furious with himself.

Only Billy didn't join in the laughter. He was looking at Rocky sympathetically. "Not your fault, Rocky," he said. "You wur conned twice."

Rocky looked up quickly. "Twice?"

But Billy quickly went on, "Come on, Rocky, ferget it – it's nothin' compared to rescuin' that girl. None of us could have done that. They're good at keepin' out of danger and laughin'!"

Billy had never spoken like that before, and it silenced the others, who looked ashamed – all except the Nabber.

Rocky brightened up. "Yer right. An *you* can suss the next job, Nabber, an' we'll see what *you* can do!"

The Nabber said condescendingly that he would consider it.

Then Little Chan said anxiously, "Rocky, look out here – it's Murky Evans."

And it was, leaning against the railings round the Steps into the hideout.

"We can't get out," said Billy, "can we?"

"Yer mean we're holed up here?" asked the Nabber.

Rocky looked out at Murky Evans. "He's by himself," he said. "None of the gang wid him. Has ter be distracted."

"Oh yes, give him a phone call," said the Nabber, looking worried.

"Listen, I'm the only one can distract him. Beady, can yer open der door quietly, an' I'll crawl up the Steps and come behind him suddenly.

Mind yer close the door quietly soon as I get out. I'll distract him, den youse can gerrout quick."

"How'll yer do dat?" asked the Nabber. "In my opinion, we're here until Murky Evans gives up tonight."

"Just thought," Rocky said to the Nabber, grinning because he was on top again. "Der's another thing we could do wid dat cotton wool – stop your mouth with it."

Beady checked that Murky Evans was looking towards Number 3, St Catherine's Square, then opened the door of the hideout very quietly. Rocky crawled out, and when Beady had shut the door he crept up the Steps, stood up and started running past Murky Evans, who immediately grabbed him.

"Wur is he?"

"Joey? Don't know."

"Yer do – he hasn't come out."

"Well, if yer know, yer know. What'll yer do about it?" he asked.

"He'll have ter come out some time," said Murky, "so just you explain the situation to him, because I'm goin' ter get him if I have ter wait till Christmas."

Rocky looked slowly and thoughtfully round the Square, and over Murky's shoulder he saw the Nabber and Little Chan carrying Billy's trike towards the Steps, Billy following and Beady shutting the door.

"Well, have a happy one," said Rocky, and twisting out of Murky's grasp, ran towards Number 3. He was about to go in when he heard a car behind him. He turned round and was astonished. It was a Mercedes Benz, accompanied by two escorts on motor-bikes who were keeping a sharp lookout round the Square.

For a moment he wondered whether Joey had managed to rob the Bank of England, then the driver of the car got out and asked him, "Are you Rocky O'Rourke?"

"What if I am?" said Rocky defensively.

"The Ambassador would like to have a word with you. Will you come to the car?"

"The who?"

"The Ambassador whose daughter you rescued."

"It's dat, is it? Well, all right." He went towards the car, waving at Murky Evans, who was obviously startled, and shouting, "Watch it, Murky, I've got outriders!"

The man in the back seat of the car invited Rocky in and sat for a while looking at him. He was a man with a round, brown face and slightly slanted eyes with laughter lines round them. He looked jolly, but his scrutiny made Rocky uncomfortable.

"So you're the boy who helped my daughter escape. I want to thank you."

"'S all right," said Rocky. "Think nothing of it. Any time, yer know, like." He looked admiringly round the car. "Never been in nothin' like this before."

"It is not bad, eh?" The man chuckled. "Very useful to be an ambassador."

"How d'yer get to be one, but?"

"Hard work and a lot of cunning." He laughed heartily. "But my wife and I are grateful to you. We suffered, you know, and were in despair. Now we are happy – because of *you*. And I am thinking, how can I thank this boy. And I have decided to give you two things. One is this cheque, and the other is this card, which gives you a phone number. You can contact me there at any time or leave a message if you need assistance of any kind."

"Thanks very much, mister." Rocky put the card into the pocket of his anorak, and examined the cheque. "Twenty pounds? Great! Thanks."

"Two thousand pounds, Rocky."

"Yer coddin'," said Rocky.

"No. Now, what will you do with it? Can you put it in a bank? Can your father advise you?"

"He's dead. Gorra stepfather, but he's away. But der's Mr Oliver on the corner der – he's a good skin. I'll ask *him*."

"Good. But remember the phone number if you need help."

As the car began to move, Rocky shouted back through the open window, "How's yer daughter, den?"

"Getting over the experience . . ."

Don't believe this, Rocky thought, and then he had an idea and ran after the car.

"Hi, mister!"

The car stopped.

"Yer could do me a favour. Me brother wants ter get ter the station. Will yer give him a lift?"

"Of course."

"Not be a minute," and he ran into Number 3 where Joey was in front of the fire, looking tense and smoking furiously.

"Hi, Joey! Pack yer case. Can get yer out without Murky gettin' yer!"

"What yer on about?"

"Arranged a lift. Can't go into it, but yer see dat car out there? Yer'll have ter move, but. He's a mate of mine, see? And he's give me this," and he showed Joey the cheque. "So, if yer ever need a loan . . ."

Joey looked from Rocky to the cheque and back to Rocky, then he said thoughtfully, "Right. Keep it in mind," and began throwing things into his case.

Rocky placed the cheque carefully on the table to admire it, then he went to reassure the ambassador that Joey was nearly ready. In a few moments Joey appeared with his case; the chauffeur opened the door for him and he got in, looking dazed, and was driven off.

Triumphantly, Rocky went back into Number 3 to take another look at the cheque. But it was not on the table or under it. It wasn't on the sofa – it had gone. Joey had taken it he realized, furious with himself for showing it to him. And leaving it there. I'll do him for this, he decided, and he ran outside again to Murky Evans, who now had his gang with him.

"Yer want our Joey, get down ter the station quick – he went off in that car," he said.

"Right," said Murky, and he and his gang moved fast.

Almost immediately, Rocky felt guilty about shopping Joey – but Joey had really shopped *him* – all that money! He could have taken his mother and Suzie on holidays – to Blackpool and London – maybe some of them foreign places his father had told him about. He kicked angrily at the wall around the abandoned garden. Been a fool, he thought. A fool. Joey always did you somehow.

"Hi, Rocky!" It was Beady and the rest of the Cats, coming up the Steps. "What's happenin'? Murky's gone, and der was this big car an . . ."

"Everythin's been happenin'," said Rocky morosely. "Our Joey's gone and taken a cheque for two thousand pounds that was given ter me."

The Cats were silent. Beady wondered whether Rocky had gone out of his mind. Billy suspected the same thing. Then Little Chan said, awed, "That is a lot of money. How did you get it?"

"He never had it," said the Nabber. "Another one of his ideas. Never mind, we'll see yer get mental treatment."

"Yer saw a Mercedes with outriders there?"

"Thought it must be yer landlord," said the Nabber, "comin' for the back rent."

Rocky rubbed his hands through his red hair. "It was the father of that girl that was kidnapped. He's rollin' in it, and he give me the cheque for gettin' her out of that house."

"Well," said the Nabber, "*we* all deserve handouts."

"Was *me* found her, smashed the window an' got her out, not youse. Anyway, haven't got der cheque ter cash, have I? It's our Joey'll be doin' that. He's took it!"

There was an atmosphere of deep gloom about the Cats as they considered the tragedy.

"Might as well go downtown," said Rocky at last. "Had enough of dis. Comin'?"

"Listen, Rocky," said Little Chan, suddenly. "It is possible to have the cheque stopped so that Joey can't cash it. Can you get in touch with the girl's father?"

Rocky brightened up. "Yer sure about dat,

Chan? 'Cos I've got his phone number – he said ter phone him if I needed help."

"Summed *you* up all right," commented the Nabber.

Rocky turned away from him in contempt, asking, "Anybody got some small change?"

The Cats waited outside the phone box in Larkspur Lane while Rocky phoned, but when he came out he didn't look a lot happier.

"What did he say?" asked Little Chan.

"Was a machine – took a message. 'Course it'll be hours before he gets back to London."

"Stand clear of him," warned the Nabber. "He's a disaster area – and he moves as well."

"Get them up, Nabber Neville," said Rocky, raising his fists. "Had enough of you!"

"Right!" said the Nabber, measuring up.

"Leave it," said Beady. "Won't do any good."

"Have to get home," said Little Chan, and Billy and Beady thought the same. Rocky had no intention of going downtown with the Nabber and he was hungry, so he went home as well. The Nabber found himself alone in Larkspur Lane on a Saturday. He shrugged his shoulders, leant against Pa Richardson's wire frames for a while, chewing something, then went home as well.

Mrs Flanagan was frying sausages when Rocky got into the flat, and Suzie was on the sofa looking fierce.

"Wur've *you* been?" Mrs Flanagan demanded in a harassed voice. "An' wur's Joey? An' them fellers – what yer call dem? Dey've cleared off."

"Dat's right." Rocky dropped down on the sofa beside Suzie. "How's it, tatty-'ead?"

Suzie relaxed and smiled. Her face was looking a lot better. "All right, Rocky."

"Dat girl that was in der house – *she's* all right."

"Old woman in box?"

Rocky frowned. He'd forgotten about her. "She'll be all right."

"What are you two goin' on about?" demanded Mrs Flanagan. "I said wur's Joey?"

"Gone off."

"Gone off wur to, but?"

"Said der station."

"What for?" Mrs Flanagan stood with a fish slice dripping fat on the floor.

Spend my money, Rocky thought angrily, but he only muttered, "Didn't say nothin'. Just went. He'll be back." He didn't go into the business of the cheque with his mother. Would only lead to complications. "Dem sausages ready? An' is dem all we're gettin? I'm hungry."

"Der's beans. Thought we'd have a proper meal, and there's Joey goin' to miss it!"

Rocky got up. "Well, I'll just . . ."

"Yer'll not. Yer'll wait till dey're served proper. Sure he didn't say nothin', Joey?"

"He'll be wid his friends in Birkenhead." Rocky dropped back on to the sofa. "He had ter get away from Murky Evans, yer know, like."

His mother put three plates of sausages and beans on the table and sat down. Suzie started immediately with the help of her own fingers and a fork and a splash of tomato sauce. Rocky added a piece of bread and butter and ate thoughtfully, not to say sadly, considering the fate of the cheque. Mrs Flanagan ate slowly, gazing into the distance.

Suddenly she dropped her knife and fork and fell back in her chair.

"I've got the intuitions," she said.

Rocky and Suzie looked at her apprehensively. Mrs Flanagan's intuitions were well known in the family. They generally meant something awful would happen.

"What yer got the intuitions about, mam?" asked Rocky, cautiously. "Is it Joey?"

Slowly his mother turned to look at him. "No. It's about *you!*"

Rocky searched his conscience. He hadn't done much recently – only the cotton wool and smashed the window and there had been that cheque. Could his mam have got on to *that*? Suzie stared desperately at Mrs Flanagan and Rocky was worried in case she started throwing things.

"S'all right den, mam. Nothin' wrong wid me."

"I'm never wrong," said his mother. At that moment, somebody knocked on the door.

"Told yer," said Mrs Flanagan, and got up to answer it. Rocky began to think up alibis, but it was only Ellen-from-upstairs with her baby, Trevor.

"And what do *you* want?" demanded Mrs Flanagan. She and Ellen had fallen out.

"Well, Mrs Flanagan, I'm sorry, but I was just worried because *her* from Number 4 said der'd been a big car an' two motor-bikes at your place this mornin', and I was worried about what might have happened, yer know, like. Even though I did say I'd never cross your doorstep again."

Mrs Flanagan was stunned. "What yer mean? A big car and . . . It's me intuitions!"

"Can't be, mam, but," said Rocky, finishing off

his meal. "It happened before yer had yer intuitions." And he saw difficulties ahead.

"Well, I'll not bother yer," Ellen said, but Mrs Flanagan changed her mind.

"No. Come in, Ellen, an' have a cup of tea. Sorry we fell out. Now what's all this about?"

Ellen came in nervously and said, "Sorry, Rocky," quietly, and Rocky immediately knew that Ellen had seen everything from upstairs and it wasn't just a report from the woman in Number 4.

"Now," said Mrs Flanagan, pouring out tea, "what's it all about?"

"Was nothin', mam," said Rocky. "Was about a girl that was kidnapped and I helped her to escape. But it's secret, mam."

"I don't believe in that," said Mrs Flanagan. "Yer gettin' like yer father – wandering."

"Yer can ask dem down on Larkspur. Did happen. An' her father come round in his big car ter thank me, see? Dat's all. But it's *secret*!"

Ellen was all ears.

"Well, I wish I'd been in. An' yer should of told me."

"Was nice of him," said Ellen.

"Was. An' so I asked him if he'd take Joey ter the station so he could escape from Murky Evans an' der Crown Street Gang, an' he did."

"Well," Mrs Flanagan concluded, "he's paid yer back for helping his daughter."

"Dat's right, mam," said Rocky.

"Dat's right," said Ellen. "Be in der *Echo*!"

"But if it was *my* child being kidnapped an' helped to escape an' I had money, I would of done more."

"Dat's right, mam," said Rocky, giving up, "yer would of." And he sat back to drink his tea and read his comic, while Suzie finished eating and Ellen-from-upstairs and his mother talked.

He began to wish he *was* Enok, the Doomlord's son, and could have been warped into something that could have gone after Joey and got the cheque back. And his mam's intuitions *had* been right – if a bit late. Had been Joey and the cheque. He hoped Murky had got Joey.

Then he thought it didn't matter really, because he wouldn't have known what to do with the cheque and maybe Mr Oliver wouldn't either.

CHAPTER

11

Saturday morning, a week later, the Cats' team headed for Prinney Park in their colours of red, which ranged in fact from orange through red to pink, with Rocky bouncing the ball around as they ran. The Nabber was the only immaculate one and he came behind them, dignified, at his own pace.

"Hi, Mr Oliver," Rocky shouted when they arrived. "How's it?"

"What do *you* think?" asked Mr Oliver rather sternly, directing Rocky's attention to the Bone-Breakers. They were all warming up. "Have yer work cut out, I think."

"Right," said Rocky. "Come on, Cats. Warming up. Come on, Nabber, get yer skates on. Yer the slowest thing since dey invented tortoises!"

The Nabber maintained a silent dignity.

Mr Oliver was proved right. Rocky informed Blair that Mr Oliver was their coach and the referee. Blair looked doubtful about that, but Rocky said, "Yer can trust him. He's impartial. Was a star player for Liverpool."

"Thank you, Rocky," said Mr Oliver. "So we'll get started. And don't say I didn't warn yer." That bothered Rocky.

The Bone-Breakers were a good team. They worked together and passed like nobody's business and took the ball from the Nabber, who was dribbling it intently towards their goal, and got it right through Beady's defence between the two anoraks that marked the Cats' goal.

"Told yer," muttered Mr Oliver.

"Yer hopeless, Nabber," said Rocky angrily. "Wake yourself up. Yer couldn't dribble round a baby in a pram! An' keep the ball on the right. They're weakest there."

They did better then. Little Chan got the ball to the Nabber, who dribbled rather more successfully and got it to another Cats' player who got it to Rocky, who scored. But after that it went to pieces and the Bone-Breakers scored another two. After half-time Chick's Lot appeared and stopped to watch and give their comments.

"Kittens' play-time!" shouted Chick.

"Wur's yer mams, but?" yelled Spadge.

Disturbed by all of this, the Nabber scored an own goal and Chick's Lot roared. "Der wind's against him!" they shouted, and, "Try it again backwards!" and, "Give him a compass!" And when Rocky was tackled just as he'd got ready to score, they shouted, "Hit him with yer handbag!"

"Had enough of this," muttered the Nabber.

"Me as well," said Rocky.

"Take dem out?"

"Yer on. Come on, Cats!" Rocky shouted and led the attack.

The Bone-Breakers were as astounded as Mr Oliver when the Cats threw themselves on Chick's Lot. Mr Oliver blew the whistle. "S'over," he said to the Bone-Breakers. "Finished." And they all watched the bodies rolling over, punching each other and shouting.

Suzie, with a large stone in her hand, was jumping up and down, and screaming. It was when Chick got on top of Rocky and started punching him that Suzie went forward and hit Chick hard on the head with her stone. Rocky pushed Chick off and staggered to his feet.

"Better stop this," Mr Oliver said.

The Bone-Breakers agreed and moved in. Chick's Lot, overcome by numbers, picked themselves up and departed. The Cats picked *themselves* up, looking dazed.

"I'll have ter have a word wid yer about dis, Rocky," said Mr Oliver.

"Wasn't *my* fault, but. Didn't start it." Rocky rubbed his nose, which was bleeding.

"I can't coach or referee in such circumstances. Sorry," Mr Oliver added to Blair.

"Wasn't our fault, but!" Rocky shouted after him.

"Yer didn't have to," said Blair.

"Dey was puttin' us off playin'," protested Rocky.

"Tell yer what, Rocky," said Blair, "we'll have ter find somewhere else ter play."

"Yer right. But we've never had nothin' like dis before."

Mr Oliver departed and so did the Bone-Breakers and the Cats followed, slowly and subdued.

"If my father hears about this, he will not let me play again," said Little Chan.

"I'm not playin' again anyway," said the Nabber. "Safer playin' chicken across Prinney Boulevard."

Beady and Billy, still recovering from the fight, said nothing and the Cats separated quite quickly.

"Bad, Rocky," said Suzie. "Bad. Swine."

"Hope yer didn't do Chick a serious injury," said Rocky.

They went into the Square, and there was the Mercedes and the two outriders and Mrs Flanagan on the doorstep, looking quite wild.

"Dey want yer!" she shouted. "Wur've yer been? What've yer been up to? Yer a mess!"

Rocky went to the car. What with Suzie's bruised face and his bleeding nose, they *were* a mess. But the Ambassador in the car only said, "Are you all right?"

"Just some football."

"I got your message. And the cheque was stopped. All right?" He smiled at Rocky's disappointed face. "But I'll invest the money for you in your name – I think that would be better, but this might be more immediately useful." And he handed Rocky four five-pound notes.

"Thanks very much. That's great. But could I have another five for me sister? – she did try ter stop them draggin' yer daughter into that house an' der's an old woman next door who tried to help . . ."

"What about this? Another five-pound note, ah? All right?"

Rocky grinned. "Thanks very much! See yer!"

"You will. And by the way that brother of yours didn't get out at Lime Street Station – he asked to be dropped off earlier." And the car reversed and departed.

Rocky was stunned. Murky would blame *him* – think he'd lied to save Joey. Murky would be after *him*!

"What's goin' on?" demanded his mother when

he went into the flat. "What yer up to? Trouble, in't it? An' how did yer get yerself inter that mess?"

"Just playin' footy."

"Well, yer can stop it and get cleaned up. An' I'm sick of cleaning yer clothes!"

"Here, mam, here's a fiver – buy yerself a new hat. An' *there's* a fiver, Suzie."

"Yer've been robbin' a shop!"

"No, mam. Was the feller – the one I helped his daughter to escape – he was up from London again so just been round ter thank me."

"Well, and so he should. How much more yer got?"

"Tell yer some time."

"Well, I'll just go upstairs and tell Ellen!"

"Come on, Suzie, we'll get cleaned up an' go an' find the old woman."

Just as they were leaving the Square, somebody shouted, "Rocky!"

Rocky twisted round, prepared for Murky, but it was John, the boy who had had the paper round before him. John looked serious.

"Got a message from Murky from one of his gang. Don't understand it, but he says he won't forget you."

"Wur's he now, but?"

"Got into a punch-up last week at a pub near Lime Street Station. Think he'll get jail."

Rocky relaxed. "Well, pass on my sympathy, and I hope he has a long visit there. Couldn't be in a safer place from my point of view. Thanks, John. Yer a good skin."

"But, Rocky – Murky – he might . . ."

"Not for a long time! Come on, tatty-'ead!"

It took some time before they found an empty shop with its windows broken and inside a long cardboard box and an empty supermarket trolley.

They were silent and puzzled.

"Gone, Rocky," asked Suzie. "Gone where?"

"Don't know," said Rocky, but he didn't like the look of things.

There was a fruit shop next door, and Rocky went in and spoke to the Indian owner. "Hi, mister, have yer seen an old woman in a long black coat round here?"

"Yes, she *was* here."

"Wur's she gone to?"

The Indian hesitated and glanced at Suzie. "She was taken ill and is in hospital. Very ill – heart."

Rocky hoped Suzie had not taken this in, but outside the shop she started to cry. "Dead, Rocky," she sobbed. "Woman dead – good woman."

"Not dead," though he thought she was. "In the hospital. An' yer've been in one yerself, haven't yer? Wasn't bad?"

Suzie thought about it and brightened up. "Warm," she said, "an' flowers, an' pictures, an' food."

"Dat's right. So yer needn't worry an' tell yer what," he went on in a burst of enthusiasm, "we'll get some ice-cream an' then we'll go an' see if we can find her in the hospital."

Then he had to watch Suzie muttering, "Good", over every mouthful of ice-cream while he wondered how he was going to find which hospital the woman in the cardboard box was in. Still, Suzie would enjoy the search.